JOKER'S WILD
VEGAS UNDERGROUND, BOOK 5

RENEE ROSE

BURNING DESIRES

Copyright © February 2019 Joker's Wild by Renee Rose

All rights reserved. This copy is intended for the original purchaser of this book ONLY. No part of this e-book or paperback may be reproduced, scanned, or distributed in any printed or electronic form without prior written permission from the author. Please do not participate in or encourage piracy of copyrighted materials in violation of the author's rights. Purchase only authorized editions.

Published in the United States of America

Renee Rose Romance

Editor: Maggie Ryan

This e-book is a work of fiction. While reference might be made to actual historical events or existing locations, the names, characters, places and incidents are either the product of the author's imaginations or are used fictitiously, and any resemblance to actual persons, living or dead, business establishments, events, or locales is entirely coincidental.

This book contains descriptions of many BDSM and sexual practices, but this is a work of fiction and, as such, should not be used in any way as a guide. The author and publisher will not be responsible for any loss, harm, injury, or death resulting from use of the information contained within. In other words, don't try this at home, folks!

ACKNOWLEDGMENTS

My enormous gratitude to Aubrey Cara for her beta read and for Maggie Ryan's fabulous editing. I love you guys!

Thanks also to the amazing members of my kinkster Facebook group, Renee's Romper Room.

WANT FREE RENEE ROSE BOOKS?

Go to http://subscribepage.com/alphastemp to sign up for Renee Rose's newsletter and receive a free copy of *Theirs to Protect, Owned by the Marine, Theirs to Punish, The Alpha's Punishment, Disobedience at the Dressmaker's* and *Her Billionaire Boss*. In addition to the free stories, you will also get special pricing, exclusive previews and news of new releases.

CHAPTER 1

unior

IT'S SUPPOSED to be a civil meeting after dark at Caffè Milano.

Trouble is, you never know when you're dealing with Russian *mafiya*. Fucking unpredictable feral bastards.

We're here today to talk territory. They've been encroaching on our neighborhoods. Moving drugs. Working prostitution with females I suspect are enslaved.

I don't give a shit what they do anywhere else, and fuck knows we don't have much business in our old neighborhoods anymore, but I consider it a Family obligation to keep them clean. Keep the fucking Russians out of them.

We meet in the open, at a sidewalk cafe in Cicero. We

1

call it the old neighborhood, kinda like how my father's generation used to refer to the Old Country.

We're in the business of lending money, same as always. It's legit, unless you count the beatdowns that come with not making payments on time. These days, business has grown to huge proportions and we're now living in mansions in the suburbs. Which doesn't mean I don't care about what happens in my territory.

I see one of the younger *bratva* sitting at a table—Ivan, I think. Vlad, their leader, doesn't seem to be there.

Cazzo. I don't like the way this is going.

My brothers, Gio and Paolo, and I get out of the Range Rover, along with our soldiers, Mario and Luca. We're all armed, although we don't make a show of it by openly carrying weapons.

"Where's Vlad?" I ask Ivan. Gio comes with me, the other three hang back, as arranged.

Ivan shrugs, looking bored. "Coming."

The girl working the counter—a slouchy millennial in skinny jeans and a fitted top comes out. I recognize her but I don't know her name. She's the granddaughter of the original owner, Luigi Milano, my father's friend.

"Mr. Tacone." She greets me but her face is anything but friendly. In fact, her lips are drawn in a thin line and a muscle jumps in her jaw. She darts a glance at the Russian and back at me like she's afraid of having both of us in her place at the same time.

I named Caffè Milano as the meeting location because I consider it friendly territory for us, but I wonder if, with the new generation, things have changed. Maybe they've made deals with the Russians.

I should be angry by the thought, but it registers as a low buzz, hardly an interest.

"Can I bring you anything? An espresso? Cannoli?"

"Get lost," the Russian snaps and she visibly jerks, and when her gaze swivels back to me, there's pleading in it.

Fuck.

Whatever the Russians are doing here, she's not down with it.

Which means I still have a problem.

"Espresso," I say, wishing I could think of her name. I remember her running around here as a little girl back when my dad used this as a meeting place. Marissa? Faith? Fuck, I have no idea.

She stands there a second longer—way too long for a normal server, and now I'm positive there's a problem.

"Get. Lost." The Russian looks dangerous.

She throws one last glance my way and heads inside.

Gio's elbow presses subtly but firmly against my arm. He's telling me something, too. I sense Paolo shift behind us.

Fanculo, this thing is going sideways. It's a trick. An ambush.

I glance through the large plate glass window. Every seat near the window is taken. Unusual for this time of night. Caffè Milano is more of a daytime deli. They stay open until evening, but people aren't usually hanging around. I notice every customer in the place has his head bent as if to obscure my view of his face.

Ivan stands up and my hand inches toward the Walther PPK at the back of my waist. "Let's go inside."

"I don't think so," Gio answers for me, whipping out his gun.

And just like that, the thing explodes.

Shots ring out from fucking everywhere. Some come from inside the cafe, shattering the glass. Some come from our guys behind me. Gio and the Russian on the sidewalk fire at each other.

I throw the table through the glass, shattering it with explosive force to clear the view, then aim and shoot at a wounded Ivan at the same time he hits Gio.

Gio grunts and staggers backward, clutching his gut.

No. *No!* Not Gio. *Fuck!*

Things go slow-motion for me. I grab Gio's gun from his hand and shove him into Paolo and Mario. "Get him to the car!" I shout as I aim at the heads ducked down below the window. I pull the triggers.

One. Two. Three dead. I'm shooting with both hands like I'm in a motherfucking movie.

I slam my foot into the door to kick it open and walk through. Four. Five down. I swing the guns around, looking for movement. Luca enters behind me, gun drawn, late to the show.

Something moves behind the counter and I pivot the muzzle of my Beretta. Luca aims too. It's the Caffè Milano girl.

Fuck. Can she be trusted not to squeal? I hold the gun steady as I make my decision.

"She's a witness," Luca murmurs, like I don't already know. But we don't kill the innocent. My mind spins on how loyal her family was, and whether that bond still holds.

Her eyes fill with tears. "Mr. Tacone…"

Merda. I shove both guns in my pockets. She's loyal. She wanted to warn me, I'm sure of it.

"No, not Tacones," I tell her firmly. I sweep a hand around the room. "Russians."

"Right," she nods shakily. "*All* Russians."

Smart girl.

"Give me five minutes before you call 911."

"Got it." Her head's still wobbly on her neck.

I back toward the door. "I'm good for the damages." I jerk my head toward the window, the bullet-riddled interior.

Tears spill down her cheeks as we leave and jump into the running car.

Paolo takes off, driving fast but easy-like. Not squealing tires or calling attention to us.

"Gio. Gio? Talk to me." I sit beside my brother, pressing my hand over his where he holds the wound.

"I'm hit." Gio's slumped in the back seat, blood soaked through his shirt and jacket.

"I know. Just hang in there. You're gonna be okay, you hear me?"

"Where to, Junior?" Paolo shouts from the front seat.

"My place. Then you three go pick up Desiree Lopez."

"Ma's nurse?"

"That's right. She owes me a favor. She works in Trauma at Cook County. If she's not at work, she lives on 22nd in Humboldt Park. Find her and bring her to my house."

Desiree

I BARELY NOTICE my surroundings as I walk, keys in hand, to my old but running fourteen-year-old Honda Civic. I don't see the shiny black Range Rover parked a few spaces down.

My instincts don't warn me.

Maybe they would've if I hadn't just worked a twelve-hour shift in Trauma. Maybe I wouldn't have just plodded out to my parking garage, brushing off the security guard's offer to walk me to my car.

Not until two big guys in trench coats get out of it and come right for me.

Oh God. This is it. I'm about to be raped and killed.

I freeze for one second, heart pounding, then dart forward, racing to jump in my car before they can reach me.

"Hold it!" One of them yells and they both lunge, one blocking my driver's side door, the other coming after me. "Desiree Lopez?"

My brain can't even compute how they know my name. I open my mouth to scream, but the guy claps a hand over my mouth. "Quiet." His terse command comes out deep and scratchy. He smells of cigar smoke. He takes my purse from my shoulder, pulls out my wallet and looks at my I.D. "Yeah, it's her."

Adrenaline pumps through my veins. I know what they say. If someone drags you to a car, you're not going to come back alive, so fight for your life. I elbow my kidnapper, turn my head to bite his hand.

But it's useless. He mutters a curse in some other language and tightens his hold. All my weight thrown around, all my twisting and writhing is nothing to him. He picks me up and carries me forward.

His buddy comes up behind us and presses a gun to my ribs. "Enough with the struggle. Get in the car." They haul me into the back of the Range Rover, sandwiched between the two men. One of them strips me of my purse as the vehicle takes off.

A bag drops over my head and I renew my fight, but they control me easily, each one taking a wrist and pinning them down by my sides.

"Yeah, we got her," one of them says. At first I think he's talking to the driver, stating the obvious, but then I realize he must be on a phone. "See you there."

"Wh-what's going on?" I warble.

No one answers me.

The phone call gives me pause. They wouldn't call someone to say they had me if their intent was to rape and kill, would they?

They would if they're devil worshippers who require a virgin sacrifice.

Not that I'm a virgin. Or that my theory is likely.

"I don't know what you want, but, please. Please let me go."

Again, no one bothers answering.

The Range Rover drives fast—and the way it only briefly slows, I'd bet they are rolling through stops or red lights, making me plow into the men beside me when it turns.

We drive long enough for me to get good and scared.

For my breath to shudder in and out on silent sobs. No tears, though. I must be too afraid to let go.

And then we stop. The asshole on my right drags me out of the car, and I stumble for my footing, the blackness of the sack over my head stealing my sense of balance as well as my sight.

The surroundings are quieter—not a city street anymore, but still a sidewalk under my feet.

"What the fuck are you doing?" An angry male voice demands in a low voice, drawing closer with each word. "I told you not to hurt her."

"She's not hurt, just scared." The voice beside me is low, too. We must be someplace people would hear us if they raised their voices. A neighborhood?

"Let her go." The bag flies off my head.

I open my mouth to scream, but the sound dies on my lips when I blink up at the pair of sharp, dark eyes above the stubbled masculine line of a powerful jaw belonging to my former employer.

Junior Tacone.

Shit.

My galloping heart slows, reverses direction, takes off again.

"Junior." I call him by the name his mother used when I worked in her house, forgetting the "Mr. Tacone," forgetting to show respect.

And then, because I had actually been attracted to this man last time I saw him—had thought maybe he had a thing for me, too—and I just had the shit scared out of me, I slap his face, hard.

The men beside me growl and grasp my arms again.

"Let her go." He takes my forearms instead, pulling me into him. Through his long wool coat, the firmness of his large body presses back at me. His dark gaze is commanding. Intense. "I'll let that slide, this time. Because they scared you."

A shiver runs up my spine. *He'll let that slide.*

This time.

Like ordinarily, there are consequences for slapping the mob boss.

Of course there are.

"Now, come inside, I need your help."

I look up the sidewalk at the huge house illuminated by streetlights. It's not his mother's Victorian brick where I worked for three months as a home healthcare nurse after her hip surgery.

Must be his?

I try to pull my wrist from his grasp. "No. You can't just, just… *kidnap* me and tell me to come inside because you need my help."

He shifts his grasp and tips his head toward the house. "Let's go." He doesn't even bother answering my argument. And I suppose that's because I'm dead wrong. He *can* just kidnap me and demand my help. He's Junior Tacone, of the Chicago underground. He and his men have guns. They can make me do whatever they damn well please.

The relief that trickled in when I saw his handsome face ebbs back out. I may still never walk out of here. Because whatever awaits me in that house isn't going to be pretty. Or legal.

Someone's hurt and they need a nurse. That's my best

guess.

And now I'll be a witness to whatever they're trying to hide.

Is one of their members hurt? Or are they torturing someone? Need me to keep him alive so they can get something out of him?

I have no choice but to go in. I may have spunk, but I'm not willing to find out what happens if you defy the kingpin of Chicago. I fall into step beside him, hurrying to match his long strides.

He slides his grip from my wrist to my hand. His large hand warms my icy one and has a protective quality, like we're on a date.

Like I'm not his prisoner.

CHAPTER 2

unior

I'M STILL MOSTLY FUNCTIONING on autopilot. Probably in shock in my own alpha asshole way.

Even so, I know pulling Desiree into this situation was wrong.

I'm breaking one of our sacred rules—*don't involve or corrupt the innocent.*

But she was the first person I thought of and the only one I fully trust to save Gio. Yeah, we have a few veterinarian connections we've used in the past, but it's been years. They must be in their eighties now—friends of my grandfather. I don't know who we can trust anymore.

And if Gio dies, it's all on me. I'll never forgive myself. I keep questioning my judgment on not bringing him to the hospital, but if I do, the Russians' deaths will be pinned on him. Or on me. *Fuck!* —on us.

This is how my father would've handled it. We've treated bullet wounds in-house before. Just not immediate family. Paolo, Luca and Mario follow us in.

I pull Desiree into the house, jog up the stairs, still holding her hand.

She's all piss and vinegar, dragging her feet to show me her reluctance, but underneath it, I smell her fear.

Which is for the best. I need her afraid. In my line of work, fear is an integral part of business.

We reach the landing and I turn toward the guest bedroom where Paolo helped me carry Gio, who had passed out by the time we arrived.

"Oh shit." Desiree sees Gio. She strips off her coat and throws it on the floor as she runs into the room.

Relief hits me square between the eyes. Any worries I had that I'd have to coerce her to even look at him evaporate. She's already in nurse mode, zeroing in on her patient.

"Your brother."

She's met him, then.

Or maybe she just sees the resemblance.

"Let me see." She pries the blood-soaked washcloth from his wound. "Gunshot wound," she mutters. "Help me roll him to the side to check for an exit wound."

I've already noted one, but I help her see for herself.

"Good, that's good. It means we won't have to go digging out a bullet. How much blood has he lost?"

I don't know if she expects me to give an actual calculation, but all I can do is hold up the first towel he went through before the current washcloth.

"Great. That's a good sign, too. There would be way more blood if it hit anything major."

I'd already guessed at the same, but I don't disturb her process. "Tell me what you need." I lift my chin at Paolo, who's standing in the doorway. He pulls out his phone, thumb hovering over the keypad.

"A needle and thread to close the wounds. Gauze to pack them. Saline. Lots of saline—to keep them clean. I can use Everclear or some other alcohol in a pinch, but I'd really prefer saline. And I'll need IV needles—21 gauge if you can get them. And the bags and tubes. Sodium potassium for the IV. And an antibiotic. Is he allergic to penicillin?"

"No." My throat closes, a fresh rush of fear for Gio flooding me.

"Then penicillin."

"Hang on. Back up. I didn't get it all," Paolo mutters.

She repeats the list for him. "Also, any pain killer or muscle relaxant would be good, because it's going to hurt like hell for a good while."

"Got it," Paolo says.

I'm feeling better about my decision to involve Desiree by the minute. Her swift, incisive action is exactly how she won over my impossible-to-please ma when she worked for her. She's excellent at what she does.

And so very nice on the eyes, too.

Not that I dragged her here for that.

She eyes the bloody towels again. "I don't think we'll need a blood transfusion."

"If we do, you can take my blood," I say quickly. I remember getting typed when we were kids and we Tacones were all the same—O positive.

"Or mine," Paolo says. He's nearly as pale as Gio.

"Is that it for medical supplies?" I ask.

"In the trunk of my car is a med kit. I'd like to have that, too."

"Get her car somewhere safe," I tell Paolo.

"On it," Paolo mutters, leaving.

I don't have a clue where he's going to get all the shit she needs, but I know he'll figure it the fuck out, just like he somehow figured out how to find and bring Desiree. This is our brother's life on the line.

DESIREE

"GIOVANNI," I blurt, finally remembering Junior's brother's name. I met him once at his mom's house.

My heart's been beating hard since I saw him lying on the bed with a bullet wound soaking the sheets. I don't know why I care so much, but it seems worse when you know the guy.

And I guess I hardly know him, but I looked after his mom for nearly three months and she talked about her kids all the time.

His eyelids flutter open and he focuses on me and groans.

"Don't move," I warn him. "I know it hurts. Don't worry. We're going to take care of you, Giovanni."

"Gio," Junior rumbles beside me.

"He goes by Gio. Got it." I straighten and look at him. "Listen, I can't do much until you get me the supplies. I don't want to stitch the wound until I clean it. I think he's relatively stable if we don't let him move."

Junior nods. "Paolo's getting the supplies."

And since there's nothing to do but wait, I decide to make my dissatisfaction felt. "You can't just *kidnap* me anytime you need a nurse."

Junior's face goes completely impassive. He says nothing. *Nothing.*

Like he's not even going to dignify me with an answer.

I smack his chest. "Seriously."

He catches my hand and pulls it back to his chest. "Careful, doll. I said I'd let it slide last time. You hit me again, there's gonna be consequences."

A shiver runs up my spine, but it's more thrill than real fear. I know, because my panties also dampen. I love having Junior talk *consequences* with me in his deep gravelly voice while holding my hand to his chest and standing inches away.

I almost love it enough to press my luck and find out exactly what those consequences will be, but I'm not quite that stupid.

I try to shove him away and retrieve my hand but he doesn't budge and my hand stays glued where it lies.

He dips his head and pins me with a dark stare. "You take care of Gio, I'll take care of you."

Now a little trickle of fear runs through me, even though I think he's making me some kind of offer, rather than a threat. I hear the undertones of every mafia deal on TV in his words, and it freaks me out.

"I'll patch him up and stay until he's stable, but that's it. I work tomorrow at noon at the hospital."

He shakes his head. "You won't leave here until he's better. I don't care if it takes a month. Tomorrow you'll call into work and tell them you came down with the flu."

I gape at him.

Shit. I am definitely still a prisoner here.

"My mom works at the same hospital—she'll be dropping by my house the second she gets off work."

His blank mask doesn't change. "You'd better think of something, then."

My stomach drops.

"Or what?"

He cocks his head, studies me for a moment. "There's a reason we're not at the hospital, *capiche*?"

I nod.

"So think long and hard about whether you want your mom to be one of my loose ends."

My entire body flushes with ice.

That was definitely a threat.

A very scary threat.

And does that mean I'm going to be one of his loose ends, too? When my usefulness ends, will he get rid of me so I won't talk?

Ohmyfuckinggod.

I'm in deep shit here.

My knees buckle. I probably would've stumbled back except for his grip on my hand.

He pinches my chin between his thumb and forefinger to bring my eyes back to his. "You'll stay here until he's better. No contact with anyone outside. And when you walk away—you'll have enough money to buy yourself a brand new car." Junior had to give me a ride home from his mother's once when my car died in front of her house. He knows how old my car is. "Okay?"

I shove at him again, tears smarting my eyes. This time he lets me go. "No, it's not okay." I blink rapidly so he won't see me cry. "You think you have my number just because I drive a piece of shit car? You think you can just kidnap me, take control of my life and make it all right with a wad of cash?"

It's unwise of me to argue with him. Stupid, really. I don't even know if his offer of money is real, or just what he's telling me to make sure I'll do the job. I do know he can make me do it, regardless.

But I'm just winding up and can't seem to stop my bluster now. "I could lose my job, you know. I just started there—I only have one day of sick time accrued."

Junior's lips close into a flat line and for the first time I realize how lethal he looks. I've always focused on the handsome side before. But now? Now I see the visage others must see when they're pissing their pants and asking God's forgiveness of their sins before they die.

Because his expression is deadly.

"You lose your job, I'll cover you, okay? Now stop giving me shit. Your job is here for now, and I expect you to do it well."

I glare at him, but I don't dare open my mouth again.

He turns me around, back to face Gio. "Come on, doll, don't make this hard." His voice loses some of the steel, bringing in a note of coaxing. "It had to be you," he says to my back.

I resist the urge to look over my shoulder at him and ask him to elaborate.

"The second you walked in here, you knew what to do. You took charge of the situation. I don't trust anyone else with my brother's life."

Something rigid eases in my chest. "I'm sure there's plenty of other people," I mutter.

"No." He steps closer. He's right at my back, although not touching me. "It had to be you." His hands come to my waist, lightly resting there.

Tingles race up and down my spine. My quads tighten and quiver.

"I'll make it worth your while." He bends his head down to mine, his mouth close to my ear. "I promise."

I swear there's innuendo in that promise. Unbidden, a fantasy I had when I worked for his mom surfaces. One where he pushes me over the kitchen table, taking me roughly from behind while I beg him to be gentle. That fantasy doesn't seem too far off from becoming a reality now and that should terrify me. Or make me sick.

Instead, flutters take off in my belly and the urge to push him over the edge into his damnable *consequences* resurfaces.

Fortunately, I'm not that idiotic. I shove the urge back down, bury it under layers of fear and righteousness and vow to never, ever let my attraction for this man show again.

He's dangerous.

He doesn't deserve that kind of attention from me.

I can't even begin to entertain ideas like that.

CHAPTER 3

unior

"You call Nico?" Paolo stands beside me as we watch Desiree work on Gio.

It's 3:00 a.m., and she's already disinfected, stitched and packed both wounds.

"No," I bristle. You'd think fucking Nico ran this family now the way everyone looks to him. Yeah, he's the one who made the Tacones hundreds of millions. He made us legit, took us away from illegal activities just by bringing the old gambling business to a state where everything's legal.

He also had nothing to lose. He's the fourth son of Santo Tacone. He slipped away with no big expectations on his head. Very little blood on his hands. He didn't have the pressure to emulate my father's vicious ways and keep order in Chicago. Didn't have to hold *La Famiglia* and the old neighborhoods together after our father went to prison.

"We should call him."

"Why?" I snap.

Paolo shakes his head. "What if this is a big fucking mistake? *Madonna*, Junior, if Gio dies—"

"He's not going to fucking die!" I snap.

Desiree whirls at the same time and glares at Paolo. "Nobody's dying on my watch." She rubs alcohol over Gio's forearm for the IV. "If you're going to be bringing my patient down with your bad attitude, you should leave."

Cristo, I love the piss and vinegar in her. It makes my cock so hard when she picks that chin up and flashes defiance right in my face. Considering her rebellion doesn't stem from ignorance, I'd say the girl had balls of steel. If she had balls, of course.

Paolo scowls and pulls me back into the hallway, out of earshot. "Okay, I get that she knows what she's doing, but what the fuck, Junior? Did you seriously think this through?"

I gnash my teeth and don't give him an answer.

"Tell me you weren't thinking with your dick when you asked me to bring her here."

I wrap my fist in his shirt and slam Paolo up against the wall, my fear for Gio making my normally low patience level non-existent. "Shut your fucking mouth. She's here because she's good, that's it."

"Right." He's breathing hard, probably working to keep

his own temper in check. "And what happens to her when this is over, huh? You gonna get rid of her?"

I pull him away from the wall and slam him back, because I don't like him threatening her life, even in a secondhand, vague way. "No, *stronzo*. I'm gonna pay her off. Money or fear will keep her quiet. Or a combination of the two. I'll handle it."

Paolo doesn't quite meet my eye, but his jaw is set at a sullen angle. "Someone ought to call Nico."

I release him and throw my hands out, Italian style. "Be my guest." I stalk away, down the stairs to the kitchen. I can't eat, but I pour a couple fingers of scotch for myself and throw it back.

I listen for Paolo's voice on the phone with Nico, but it doesn't come. Instead, the front door slams.

My skin pricks with irritation, but I pour another finger of scotch and swallow it down. Send a text to Mario and tell him I want a glass repair company at Caffè Milano first thing in the morning. I never intended to burn that business with Family shit. I will stop by there personally to repay them for damages and make sure no one there's going to squeal as soon as I can get away. And after the dust has settled.

I don't know how long I stand there with the empty glass in my hand, but eventually I hear light footsteps coming down the stairs.

Desiree comes into the kitchen. Exhaustion shows in the circles under her eyes, the weariness around her mouth.

I pull out a fresh glass, pour another couple ounces of scotch and hold it out to her.

She stares at it for a moment, then takes it wordlessly and tosses it back. Her shudder as it goes down confirms my suspicion that she's not much of a drinker.

"Hungry?" I ask.

"Yeah, but I don't think I'll eat." She pats her hips. "Not good for the girlish figure to eat before bedtime."

"Fuck that. You worked your ass off today. Your body needs fuel."

I'm not the daddying type. Not in the least. I don't even know what makes me insist. Maybe I'm just offended by her suggestion that her curvy body isn't the most perfect figure ever made.

I walk to the refrigerator and pull it open. It's mostly full of take out boxes and ready made food like that. "You want a sandwich?" I ask. "Or there's half a calzone in here."

"You have any ice cream?" Her soft voice is right behind me, and I register it with distinct pleasure.

I throw open the freezer, happy because I know I do. I pull out a full pint of Ben & Jerry's mint chocolate cookie. I'm not big on sweets, but I bought it the other day on some weird impulse.

"Ohmygod, that's my favorite." She literally snatches the carton out of my hand and tears the top off.

My lips twist in an uncharacteristic smile as I pull open the silverware drawer and grab two spoons.

I hand her one "I like your enthusiasm, doll."

She wrinkles her nose, holding the carton of ice cream right against her chest as she digs the spoon in. She flops down in one of the kitchen chairs.

I don't have people over to my house, and when I do, I

make it a practice not to make them feel at home. So it shouldn't please me that it's so easy for her to get comfortable.

But again, this is the same character trait that won my ma over. She didn't tiptoe around the house and act stiff and formal. She ruled the roost while she was there, bossing my ma around, all the while doing an irreproachable job.

I sit down in the chair beside her and try to stick my spoon in the ice cream.

"No way." She jerks it away, angling her body to shield it from me.

I chuckle. "One spoonful. Give me a taste."

My last words hang in the air between us, taking on an erotic undercurrent. Desiree blushes a bit when she offers the carton.

I take one spoonful, savor the rich treat, and then put my spoon down.

Desiree digs into the carton like it might be taken from her at any minute and she needs to get as much in her before that happens. I watch as she mmms and groans in pleasure, my dick getting hard. Every time those full lips mold around the spoon I get jealous. I vow to buy a fucking crate of this ice cream to have on hand while she's staying here.

She doesn't stop until her spoon scrapes the bottom and then she blushes again. "Dang. This is why I shouldn't be allowed to eat before bedtime."

"You deserved it." My voice sounds rusty, which seems about right, since it's unlike me to throw out compliments or praise. Ever.

She flushes deeper, looking distinctly guilty. "I have a tendency to stress eat." She sets the carton down with one large spoonful left in it.

"I enjoyed the show." I didn't mean to say it, but it's the truth. Watching her wolf down the ice cream was damn cute. I relished her enthusiasm and clear pleasure of the dessert.

Maybe in my head I'm thinking the hedonism she displayed over the ice cream translates to the bedroom.

Not that I'm going to fuck her.

I'm *definitely not* going to fuck her.

It's bad enough I dragged her into this shit storm. I don't need to further taint her with *me*.

La Madonna knows, I ruin everything I come close to.

I scoop out the last bite with her spoon and hold it out to her. It's weirdly intimate and as soon as I do it, I realize it's too much.

"No." She shakes her head and turns her face away.

"You sure? All right." I put the bite in my mouth instead and her gaze tracks to my lips, like she enjoys watching me eat as much as I loved watching her.

She stands up, running her palms down her scrubs like they're sweaty. "So. I'm spending the night, huh?"

Right. She's not a guest, she's a prisoner. I need to make sure she understands that.

I stand, too. "You'll stay in Gio's room," I say. "That way if he needs you, you'll hear him."

Her eyebrows shoot up and I can tell she doesn't like it, but she doesn't say anything. I would put her in another guest room, but I don't trust myself with her. Lord knows I want to get my hands all over her sassy curves. Want to find out what she tastes like. What it's like to pound between her legs and make her scream.

But none of that is going to happen.

So putting her in Gio's room is definitely the best plan.

We walk up the stairs to the landing. "You got a toothbrush I can use?"

Cristo. It's like an overnight without the sex. Not something I ever do—overnights, that is.

"Uh, yeah, I think I do." I head into my *en suite* bathroom and dig out an unopened toothbrush head for my sonic toothbrush. I hand it to her with the toothpaste and point to the guest bath.

"Thanks. I'll be right back with this."

She disappears into the bathroom and I close my eyes and lean against the wall.

Maybe Paolo was right.

Maybe I was thinking with my dick when I had her dragged here.

Maybe my dick is an opportunistic fuck who doesn't give a shit who I ruin.

DESIREE

I SLEEP MAYBE THREE HOURS, which is no surprise. I put codeine in Gio's drip, but he still wakes every thirty minutes groaning.

And even though I'm dead tired, I'm too keyed up about being Junior Tacone's prisoner to be able to rest. I get up when the clock reads 6:34 a.m. and slip into the bathroom to pee.

Gio's asleep, and a peek in Junior's cracked door tells me he is, too.

It's my chance to leave. I should take it. Because even though Junior promised me a big payout for staying, I'm not sure his word is good. That might just be what he's telling me to make sure I do a good job. And when Gio doesn't need me anymore, I end up in Lake Michigan with cement shoes.

I didn't miss the threat he made if I told my mom. He'd have to get rid of her. So why would he keep me around?

He wouldn't.

No, I can't let my attraction to dangerous men keep me in danger. If I have a chance to run, I should run right now.

Gio jerks in his sleep and moans.

Shit. Maybe I should wait until his condition is more stable. What will they do without me?

No, fuck that.

It's not my problem.

I didn't volunteer for this job. They need to figure it out on their own.

I slip on my shoes and coat and hunt for my purse, which they took from me when they grabbed me at the hospital.

I search downstairs, checking closets. I even step into Junior's room and do a cursory sweep. When he snorts and rolls over, I dart back out of the room.

Screw the purse. My life isn't worth risking on the stuff in my purse.

I head back down the stairs and crack the front door. I stop at the bite of cold wind and the stare out at the graying dark.

Fuck. Should I leave?

If I do, then what? Go to the cops?

Maybe I'm nuts, but I don't have any desire to throw Junior or Gio to the authorities, even though they're surely involved in something very illegal. Probably deadly.

But if I don't go to the cops, what stops Junior from just grabbing my ass off the streets again and dragging me back here? And then I'm sure I'll forfeit the money he promised, which I desperately need.

To add to my dilemma, if I walk out this door, I don't even know where to go. I don't have a car or a phone. It's freaking freezing out and who knows how far we are from public transportation. The neighborhood looks ritzy —like Oak Park or some other neighborhood named after a tree.

"Shut the door."

I jump and gasp at Junior's angry voice coming down the stairs. I freeze, unable to make myself bolt out the door, or obey him and shut it. The indecision that kept me there for the last eighty seconds still has me paralyzed.

"I said, *shut it.*" His hand slaps against the door, slamming it.

I still don't move. Don't turn to look at him. Don't try to run. I guess this is what they mean by "petrified."

Tacone grabs the sleeve of my jacket and tugs it off me, tossing it onto the floor. "Where in the fuck do you think you're going?"

Oh shit. He has the most effective angry voice I've ever heard. I'm surprised I don't piss myself.

I still don't turn around—just stand facing the door like it somehow makes me safe if I can't see him.

His hand crashes down on my ass.

I gasp in surprise, but honestly, the spank is welcome.

It's not a gun. Not a wire around my neck. It's not even a backhand. It's a slap. On my ass. Simple and sexual.

He slaps me again, hard.

I bring my hands to the door to brace myself, spread my fingers, push my ass out.

I hear Junior's breath rasp out in a rush. He grunts and reaches up to capture my hands, stacking one wrist over the other and pinning them above my head as he rains stinging smacks all over my ass and the backs of my legs.

My heart pounds against my chest. It hurts and I'm still frightened, but I'm getting more and more turned on by the second.

This is like a scene out of my fantasies. Okay, they never involved spanking, but they totally involved Junior dominating me. Bending me over the couch and forcing me to have sex, or shoving me to my knees and making me suck his cock.

Being on the receiving end of a spanking at his hands definitely fits in the same category.

He stops spanking, his breath at my ear. We both pant like we ran a lap around the block. He hasn't released my wrists and I love how it feels to be captured by him. My body reacts to it before I can stop myself. I toss my head back, push my ass against his body.

To my disappointment, he releases me and steps back. "Go upstairs to my room."

Ms. Bluster makes a full appearance. I whirl and put my hands on my hips. "What for?"

His gaze is heavy-lidded. He's standing there in a white undershirt and his boxer briefs, which doesn't make him seem the slightest bit vulnerable. No, the way he fills them out—chest and shoulder muscles stretching the cotton shirt, cock tenting the briefs—he's as commanding as he is in a suit. "I'm not done punishing you." He jerks his chin toward the stairs, in a silent repetition of his command.

My pussy clenches but I can't seem to drop the attitude. I cock a hip. "What does the punishment entail?"

He moves quicker than I would think possible for such a big guy. One second I'm standing there, facing off to him, the next I'm over his shoulder being carried swiftly upstairs. His hand claps down on my ass. I kick my legs and squirm because resistance is part of my fantasy.

He brings me into his bedroom and kicks the door shut, then tosses me to the middle of the bed.

I'm out of breath, mostly excited, a little scared. So far he hasn't hurt me, unless you count slapping my ass, which I don't. Yeah, it still stings, but I remember from spankings as a kid, that will go away in less than a half hour.

I watch, fascinated, as he pulls off my shoes, then yanks my scrubs down my hips and off my legs.

I automatically move to tug my top off and toss it on the floor with the rest of my stuff. I may appear a little too eager. I haven't had sex in over three years. I'm just thanking God I'm wearing matching bra and panties—a red satin and lace set that look great against my caramel skin.

"*Cristo*," he mutters, eyes black, nostrils flaring. He stares at my body with hunger. "You always wear these sexy little lace numbers under your scrubs?" He climbs over me, pushing me to my back and pinning my wrists above my head. "It's a good thing I didn't know that when you were working at my ma's." He straddles my hips, the savage lines of his face hovering over mine.

"Now listen carefully, little girl. You got one chance to say no if you don't want your punishment to involve me shoving my cock into one of your sexy-as-fuck holes."

His words shock me and my body jerks beneath his, but it's not with fear. It's from a kick of lust.

Still, I'm a fighter. Always have to show resistance. I lick my lips. "What's my punishment if I say no?"

He pulls back slightly and I'm almost sorry I asked. "I put my dick away, spank your ass some more and send you back to Gio's room to do what you're told."

Do what I'm told. I'm sure on some level that offends me. It's just not making it through to my brain at the moment.

"And if I say yes?"

A devilish glint lights up his eyes. "You're gonna end up with me pounding into you until you're good and sorry. *And then* I'll spank your ass and send you back to Gio's room to do what you're told."

I wriggle on the bed, rolling my hips beneath his, desperate for some friction on my clit. My entire body is lit up with need. Soaked with desire. "I'll take the second option." I hardly recognize my breathy voice.

His eyes gleam with what looks like satisfaction. "Yeah?"

"Do I get to pick which hole?"

His lips twist into a wicked smirk. "Oh no, baby." He flips me over to my belly. "This is punishment. That means it's my choice."

Again, rockets of desire shoot through me. This is exactly what I wanted. The fodder of all my fantasies.

He unhooks my bra in the back and pulls it off me, then pulls my wrists behind my back and ties them with it. My panties come off next, and he pulls my hips up until I'm resting on my knees with my face and shoulders still mashed into the bedcovers. He runs a hand over my ass. "You look so good in my handprints." He smacks my ass, then rubs. His fingers dip between my legs and he makes a rumble of satisfaction at what he finds there.

"Now tell me, baby." He circles my clit. "What made you so wet? Your spanking? Or knowing you're about to get fucked?" He slaps my pussy. "Or is it being tied up and at my mercy?"

I don't answer. I'm actually not sure I'm capable of speech. Plus, it seems like a rhetorical question.

It earns me a flurry of hard spanks. "I asked you a question, doll."

"Ohh-oh," I moan as he returns to rubbing my clit. He's rougher this time and I'm already starting to get close to climax, just from a few spanks and rubs.

"Hmm?" He slaps me five times in the same exact spot and I yelp and list away.

"All of it," I mumble into the covers.

"All of it," he muses. "Let's test that." He starts spanking, hard and fast. Just spanking. No rubbing. No fondling. It gets intense and I start to twist and whimper a little.

He slaps between my legs.

I cry out.

He rubs over my slit. "Mmm. Yeah. Spanking definitely makes you wet, doesn't it, doll?" He slaps my pussy again.

It feels so good—even though it startles me. Even though it stings and sends nervous flutters to my belly. I want more of it. Need more of it.

I spread my knees wider, sink into the position, offering it to him.

He curses in Italian and spanks me light and fast between the legs. *Slap-slap-slap-slap.*

I cry out.

He pinches my clit. "Don't come, baby. This is punishment, remember?"

Best. Punishment. Ever.

I'm halfway to an orgasm already. Maybe even closer. My body's feverish, desperate.

Junior grips my thighs and pulls my ass cheeks apart, licking me from clit to anus.

I shriek at the sensation. At the taboo of having my anus licked.

Junior chuckles at my reaction. "I should fuck your ass, shouldn't I?" He pushes against the tight ring of muscles, massaging my back hole. I tighten against the intrusion, squeezing my eyes shut. "I think your disobedience merits a good ass fucking."

I shake my head, rubbing my face in the bedspread. "No, please." I don't know if I'm damning myself further by letting him know I don't want it, but I am a total anal virgin. And I'm dying to feel him between my legs. "My pussy. Please. I haven't had sex in so long." I know it sounds pathetic, and it hurts my pride to admit it, but maybe he'll take mercy on me and give me what I need.

"Is that right?" Junior yanks the binding off my wrists and flips me over onto my back. "You need my cock in here?" He plunges his thumb into my pussy, grinding into my clit with his palm.

I arch, thrusting my hard nipples toward the ceiling. "Yes. Please, Junior."

Still pumping his thumb in and out, he grips his cock with the other hand and pulls it from his boxer briefs.

I prop myself up on my elbows to see better.

His grin is feral. "You're so fucking beautiful, doll."

Beautiful.

Huh.

I haven't felt beautiful in a long time. I've got this extra twenty pounds I can never get off, and I'm always stressed out of my mind with worry over finding Jasper. But Junior doesn't seem like the kind of guy who says stuff just to be nice. And the way he's looking at me, I actually think he means it.

"Do you have a condom?" I'm surprised at how shy I sound. It's not like me at all.

His answer is soft, his gaze indulgent. "Yeah." He keeps

stroking his cock and me at the same time. "I'll find one." He pulls his thumb out of me like it kills him and pads to the *en suite* bathroom. He returns with a *fistful* of condoms. I guess he really does plan on pounding me until I'm good and sorry.

He tosses them on the bed and rips one open with his teeth. I watch, fascinated, as he peels his shirt off over his head. He's all burly man—hairy chest, a tattoo covering his right pectoral and shoulder. He shoves his briefs off, too, and rolls the condom over his impressive manhood.

"Spread those legs for me, baby. Spread 'em wide and hold them there."

I open my legs spread-eagle, feet pointed toward the ceiling.

"That's it." He lines the head of his sheathed cock up with my entrance. "You hold them there until I say. *Capiche?*"

I rack my brain to remember the right answer. "*Capito!*" I blurt and his eyes light up, a shadow of a smile appears on his face. He collects my wrists and pins them above my head again, then pushes into me.

I groan at the sensation of him filling me, shoving inside. It's been way too long since I've had sex, and I don't remember it feeling this good. I rock my hips up to meet his thrusts, careful to hold the spread-eagle position. It's sort of ridiculous and I feel like some kind of sex doll, but that's exactly what works for me. I love the degradation of it, the suggestion that this might be arduous, rather than pleasurable for me.

I start making all kinds of sounds. I've never understood how people can have sex and not shout at the top of their lungs. I can't help all the noise that comes out of my throat—the cries, the moans, the unintelligible words. I beg, plead, coax. I show my appreciation with every honest sound.

"*Fanculo*," Junior mutters, pounding harder, sweat beading at his hairline.

True to his promise, he fucks hard. Each thrust rams deeper. If he didn't keep yanking me back, my head would smash into the headboard.

His hand flashes out and slaps my right breast.

I squeal in offended surprise, but he squeezes it, leans over and flicks his tongue over my nipple, all the while riding me like we're in a horse race.

"Junior," I gasp.

The strain of holding back shows on his face, but he still manages to cock a brow. "You feeling good and sorry?"

I let out a hysterical laugh. "So sorry. So damn sorry. Please, Junior."

Instead of bringing us to a finish, he pulls out.

"No!" I protest.

He rolls me to my belly. "Spread, baby."

I spread my legs. He grips the back of my neck, like he's holding me down, and enters me from behind.

It's so good, I swear I nearly pass out. Every stroke is heaven on wheels.

I turn my face to keep from suffocating in the blankets, and he rides me hard from behind, his loins against my ass, as he thrusts in so deep.

"Junior!"

"Fuck, yeah, baby. Come all over my dick now. Squeeze me tight, doll."

I clench my muscles around his cock and he shouts something in Italian, slams in with enough force to bang the bed against the wall once, twice, three times. On the fourth, he stays deep inside me and comes.

My internal muscles flutter around his cock, squeezing and releasing as I come, too. I'm lightheaded. I'm lost.

And then, for some unknown reason, I'm crying.

~

Junior

Sonofabitch.

Desiree's beautiful back shakes with sobs and I nearly lose my shit. I roll her over, doing my best to keep my hands gentle when urgency makes me want to yank and tear.

"Desiree. Baby. Fuck." I gather her into my arms as she tries to hide her face in her hands.

Merda.

"I didn't mean to break you, doll. I really didn't."

It's exactly what I was trying not to do. It's why I went in hot and fucked her instead of turning on the ice and scaring the shit out of her with threats or force.

What am I saying? I didn't even mean to fuck her. I didn't know what to do—all I knew was that the usual shit I spew to people when I'm threatening the lives of the people they love wouldn't come out. So I smacked her ass.

And then she spread her palms out on the door and thrust her hips back like she liked it, and I was a goner.

But I must've misread her cues.

Something went terribly wrong because now she's hiccupping and mopping up tears like she can't stop.

She struggles to sit up. "It's good. I'm good." She wipes her tears with both fingers. "I don't even know why I cried. Just the release, you know? I'm overtired, and this has been stressful and"—she waves her hand, a rueful twist of her full lips—"it all came out. I'm sorry, this is so embarrassing."

"Embarrassing? Fuck that." I won't let her go even though she's fighting for sovereignty. Instead, I pull her around to straddle my lap, hold her tight against my chest. "You're really okay?" I stroke up and down her bare back.

She gives a watery laugh. "Yes. Can we please forget this happened?"

"Stop," I command. "I don't give a shit if you bawl your eyes out every time you come. Hell, I don't care if you puke. As long as I know it was good for you."

She laughs against my neck, still hiding her face there. "It was good."

"Too rough?" I'm still shell-shocked from thinking I hurt or scared her.

"No." Her lips move against my neck. Is she kissing me? "I liked it."

I keep holding her tight, partly because I love the feel of so much soft skin up against mine. But also because I figure she needs to be held even if she's trying to pull her shit together and pretend nothing happened. And I'm not oblivious to the fact that I caused the stress she had to release through her tears.

"I had this fantasy..." I hear her say in a very small voice. Like she's telling me a secret, here in the dark. "Back when I worked for your mom. I used to imagine you forcing me to have sex."

I somehow manage to not stiffen. She's talking about a *fantasy*. It doesn't mean she believes I would actually force a woman to have sex with me.

"You get hot for a little violence in the bedroom, doll?"

She leans her chin on my shoulder. Her bare breasts push against my chest. "I don't know. Yeah, I guess so. I mean, just a fantasy, right? Of course I would never want to be forced in real life. And any guy who did that—"

"Yeah, yeah," I interrupt. I'd rather stick with her fantasies than discuss rape. I pull her hips against mine. Her cunt is still slick with her juices and it rubs over my cock, getting me semi-hard again.

Her lips find the place where my shoulder meets my neck again. This time I'm sure it's a kiss or love bite or whatever.

"I can't even believe I'm telling you. It's just that you kinda just made it all come true. In a good way," she rushes to add. "I don't mean I really felt forced."

My dick lengthens. "Well—" I keep stroking her back, palming her ass, consuming her. "I'm happy to act that fantasy out with you over and over again." I squeeze both her ass cheeks roughly, lifting and lowering her slowly over my cock. "Let's just say while you're in this house, you might be subject to forced fucking any time I feel like it."

Her breath catches and she goes still, like she's thinking it over.

"We'll need some kind of signal, I guess," I suggest. "So I know if you really *don't* want it."

"You mean like a safe word?" Her warble is small again, and it kinda kills me to hear her that way, because she's usually so full of confidence.

"Safe word. Right. I guess so." I don't know shit about BDSM, but a safe word makes sense.

"How about if I say...*peanut butter* if I want it to stop?"

I smile. "Peanut butter. Got it. You gonna remember that, doll? If I have you pinned down and nervous?"

"I'll remember. Will you?" she demands, her sassy attitude returning.

"Yep. Did you just agree to be my on-demand pussy for the rest of the time you're here?"

She bites my shoulder, hard enough to leave a mark. "No. You just agreed to be my gigolo."

I chuckle, stroking her soft skin. I'm not sure when I've last smiled or chuckled. But then again, I haven't had sex like that in...well, maybe ever.

Even with Gio in critical condition in the next room, the heaviness that usually hangs over my head seems temporarily lifted.

And I hate to end it, but Gio's waiting. And I need to get things straightened out with his nurse.

I ease back so I can see Desiree's face and catch her jaw in an overhand hold. "Okay, doll. We still have serious shit to talk about."

Her eyes widen.

"Why were you leaving?"

Desiree sags a bit. "I didn't leave," she insists. "I was *considering* it."

I force myself not to smile. It's so cute how she always argues with me.

"Okay. Why?"

She shrugs, a slightly mulish expression settling over her. "I'm not really sure I'm going to walk out of here alive." She lifts her chin, a direct challenge flashing in her big brown eyes.

Now it's my turn to sag. As much as her fear pisses me off, she's right to worry. She's gonna be a loose end, and if I were smart, if I were ruthless, I would make sure she didn't walk out of here and talk.

"Oh, baby." I release her jaw and let my grip trail down her throat. It's not a threat, but she swallows convulsively beneath my hand. "I don't off innocent women." I trace her jaw. "Especially not ones who work their asses off to save my brother's life." I cup behind her nape and pull her toward me to kiss her neck. "Especially not ones with little freckles on their upturned noses." I tap her nose. "I promise you'll walk away from this with the rewards you deserve. I know how to show my appreciation to the people who prove their loyalty. I'm going to take care of you, Desiree."

"Aren't you afraid I'll talk? I mean, there's a reason Gio's not at the hospital, right?"

Regret washes through me. I wish she wasn't pressing me on this. "Oh, baby, I have hundreds of ways to keep you from talking, and none of them involve putting you six feet under. But I don't want to make threats. Not with the taste of you still on my tongue. Not when you just made me come harder than I have in years."

I watch the veil of lust drop back down over her face and she writhes over my lap in an intoxicating swivel.

"So I'm gonna say this, and I'm only gonna say it once. I need you to stay here and take care of Gio. I need you to promise you won't tell anyone where you are, or who you're with. Not now or ever. And I need you to know that if you disobey me again, there will be serious consequences. *Capiche?*"

Her face goes pale and I detect a little pissed-off in her expression, but mostly she keeps it hidden. She pushes off my lap, and this time, I let her leave. "Yeah, I got it." Definitely a sullen ring to her voice.

Well, that's good. She needs to be scared of me.

I can't just fuck her into compliance, as much as I'm gonna try.

CHAPTER 4

Desiree

I YANK on my underclothing and day-old scrubs, wishing I could drop-kick Junior.

I don't know what in the hell I was thinking, making a sex arrangement with the man! I am not going through with it. I will definitely be calling *peanut butter* the first time he tries to lay his hands on me.

Junior is dangerous. I was stupid to have sex with him once.

I don't need to repeat the mistake.

I go and check on Gio, even though I refreshed his IV and meds before I tried to leave. He's still okay. No fever. Pulse is in a decent range. He's sweating a little, and I pull the blankets down to give him some air. I use the bottom sheet to roll him to his side so he doesn't get bedsores.

When I'm done, I breeze into Junior's room like I own the place and open his drawers until I find his t-shirts. He isn't around—I hear him talking on his phone downstairs. He only has a drawerful of clean white V-necks—not a single color or graphic tee to be found. I grab one, then head into the guest bathroom where I take a shower.

I make it long and steamy. There's no razor, but there's soap and shampoo, so I wash up and then just stand there under the stream of water, like I can wash the last twenty-four hours off me.

Except it's not long before I fall into thinking about the amazing sex we just had. It was hot and fantasy-fulfilling, but also more.

He called me beautiful.

He rolled with my breakdown—*held* me, even.

Some of my sourness drops away. Yes, Junior is infuriating. He's holding me prisoner here. He took unforgivable liberties with my life when he decided I'd be the best person for this job.

But he's not all bad. He can't be. He loves his brother. He loves his mom.

He's a cold-blooded killer, the voice in my head warns.

True. He practically admitted to it. *I don't make a habit out of offing the innocent.* Maybe not, but the guilty? I'm sure he serves them justice in many horrible ways.

He fixed my car, pushover me argues. *He held me when I cried.*

He fucks like a demon.

Okay, *that* is not a good enough reason.

I turn off the water and climb out, drying off with a towel I pulled from the cabinet. I put my clothes back on, except I wear Junior's t-shirt instead of the top of my scrubs.

When I come out, masculine voices rumble downstairs. I square my shoulders and play the same game I played as a home healthcare nurse: Act like I run the show around here until everyone gets on board and trusts me enough to let me do my job.

I search the closets until I find a change of sheets, which I bring to Gio's room. Junior changed out the bloody towels, but we still need to change the sheets, which show some bloodstains. I start pulling the corners off the far side, away from Gio.

"Time to call into work, doll." Junior stands in the doorway, holding up my phone. He's showered and dressed, too and looks devastating as ever in a crisp button down and slacks.

He beckons me over, which annoys the piss out of me, but I come. He hands me the phone. I start to turn away, but he catches my forearm. "Uh uh. Stay right here while you call."

I huff and roll my eyes, but my fingers tremble slightly as I take the phone because I know he's worried about me trying to signal for help. I'm not thinking of trying anything. I do believe he means to let me go when this is all over. And I'm willing to see it through. Doesn't mean I'm happy about it, or I think what he's doing is right, but maybe the money I make off this will help me finally find Jasper.

I call into my department at the hospital and make myself sound miserable. "Hey, Shelly, it's Desiree Lopez."

"Hi, Desiree. You don't sound so good."

"I don't feel so good." I force a loud cough. "I woke up this morning with that nasty flu. I can't come into work today."

"Okay, I'll let them know. Hope you feel better!"

"Thanks," I moan and end the call, then lift a defiant gaze to Junior.

His lips twitch. "Good girl. Now what are you going to do about your mom?"

I've thought about it and I have an idea. "I'm going to text her."

He reaches for the phone, like he doesn't trust me, and I yank it back to my chest, thrusting my lower jaw forward.

"I need to read it before you hit send," he warns.

"Fine." I type out a text to my mom, telling her I'd called in sick to the hospital, but I really had a home healthcare job that paid twice as much so I was going to take it for the week. I said it involved traveling with a sick patient, so I wouldn't be around, but I'd check in and call her when I got back.

I hand it to Junior without sending and he reads it. "Good thinking."

"Your highness approves?"

He hits send and lifts his brows at me. "You really gonna get mouthy with me?"

I open my lips to ask what happens if I do, but the memory of the punishment he already delivered makes me flush. My nipples tingle and burn at the memory of exactly how *punitive* he gets.

The corners of his mouth quirk slightly and I know he's read my thoughts. He pockets my phone. I scowl.

"I'm expecting way more than twice as much, you know," I tell him. "I just had to make it believable for my mom."

I watch him closely for a reaction, because this is important to me. I need to know if there really is a sizeable payout involved here. As usual, he shows nothing in his expression, just watches me back.

"You said enough to buy a new car. What are we talking about? Twenty grand? Thirty?"

He nods. "Thirty, for sure. More if you earn it." There's nothing lewd about the way he says it, but my mind instantly jumps to filthy sex and my body revs up, eager to get busy earning all the riches it can get. "Why you need it?"

I frown at the intrusive question.

"I know there's a story you don't want me to know."

Funny how any possible answer gets stuck in my throat, and I'm caught staring up at him like a trapped animal. "H-how do you know that?" I manage.

He tips his head to the side. "It's my business to read people."

So he can blackmail them.

I push that thought out of my head.

Somehow I recover from the swift pain that always accompanies thinking about Jasper. I fold my arms over my chest. "You're right. I don't want you to know."

His lips twitch and he taps my nose. "I'll find out." His words are mild. It's not a threat. And yet his certainty, and the certainty that anything in my life he wants to fuck with, he can, sends chills running down my spine.

I want to snap at him to stay out of it, but I bite my lip.

The more emotion I show, the more he's going to know this is an issue I hold close to my heart.

It's not like his knowing would do any harm—it wouldn't. But this is a subject I can't bear to talk about, even with my own mom. It fucking slays me. And I've already fallen apart once on Junior this morning. I don't plan on a repeat show today or ever.

"I had Paolo bring in some food. I wasn't sure what you like to eat, but there's plenty down there. Go and help yourself."

"After I get this sheet changed. I need you to lift." I jerk my head in the direction of the bed.

"Okay, doll." I swear I detect amusement in Junior's tone, like he thinks it's funny I'm bossing him around.

I know it's insane, but I can't help it. Bluster is what I do when I'm nervous.

I give him instructions on lifting Gio using the existing sheet so I can slip the new one underneath, and I get the thing changed out to my satisfaction. As I walk out with the soiled sheets in my arms, I pass Paolo, who I now realize is another Tacone brother. He watches me as I go, but doesn't greet me or comment.

Downstairs, I find a variety of takeout from Starbucks —a steaming latte and egg sandwich, bagels, muffins. There's also a bag of groceries sitting on the counter that hasn't been put away.

I take the liberty of unloading it.

Four pints of my favorite Ben & Jerry's. I shove back the appreciation that bubbles up. My past relationships starved me in the gifts department. Someone buying my mint cookie ice cream is no reason to go moony.

I fix myself a bagel with cream cheese and sit down to eat.

I can get through this. If we take really good care of the wound, Gio should be stable in a week. Then I'll get paid a big chunk of money, which I can use to step up the efforts to find Jasper. Find where my asshole ex has holed up with our son.

I'm doing this for Jasper.

That thought calms me. Makes it all easy. I can deal with Junior Tacone and all that comes with this job if it means getting my little boy back.

∾

Junior

"Nico and Stefano are flying in this afternoon," Paolo says, his focus on Gio, not me.

"What for?" I bristle.

"Because he's our brother!" Paolo spits back.

"And did you tell Alessia and Ma?" I demand. I already know he didn't. We Tacones have a code that involves not worrying the women of the family.

"Of course I didn't. They don't need to know. Nico and Stefano are part of business."

"Are they?"

They're not, really. We're part of their business, because *La Famiglia* put up the money to start Nico's Vegas casino and now we're all shareholders of the corporation. But Nico hasn't been part of our business in over ten years. And this outfit isn't a fucking democracy. They don't get to weigh in just on the merit of being my brothers. Neither does Paolo, for that matter. But my tenure as head of the family is by nature rocky, because technically our father is still don, and any one of the fuckers can go run to him if they think I'm fucking things up.

"Well, they understand business, anyway." Paolo shoves his hands in his pockets, in a posture of concession.

I don't answer.

"How's he doing, anyway?"

"Desiree says he's stable."

"Good."

Just saying Desiree's name has me recalling how luscious she felt under my body this morning. The beautiful sounds she made, the way she gave herself over so completely. I never in a million years dreamed I'd make some woman's fantasy come true, but knowing I can?

Is fucking hot.

And even though I was an ass to her after we talked, I have the strong urge to reward her for giving herself up to me like that. And for being her.

She appeared this morning, showered and wearing one of my t-shirts. Didn't even ask me for permission, just helped herself.

I don't know why I fucking love that about her. Maybe because Marne, my ex, is so incapable of doing anything for herself with or without permission.

But as much as I love knowing she's wearing my clothes, she's gonna need her own shit.

"Listen, you stay here and keep an eye on him, huh? I'm gonna run Desiree to her apartment to pack a bag."

Paolo nods. "Sure."

"Where did you put her car?"

"It's in your garage."

"Good. I'll be back in a couple hours. Call me if anything changes with Gio."

"I will."

"And call Vlad. We need to arrange a meeting to deal with their fucking setup. As far as I'm concerned, we're at war. Find out what the word on the street is about the Russians. I want every ear to the ground."

Paolo nods, phone already out.

I jog down the stairs and find my kitchen spotless, Desiree wiping down the inside of the refrigerator. Fuck if it doesn't get me hard, imagining enacting a scene where she's my maid and I force her to bend over and take it from her boss. Does she want role play? Or is the mafia kingpin scenario all she needs from me?

I adjust my junk and clear my throat.

"Yes?" She doesn't turn around. She doesn't jump to attention, or get nervous and babble around me like other females who work for me. This girl is totally different.

Built from a very special mold.

"Grab your coat, doll. I'm gonna take you to pack a bag."

"Yeah?" Now she turns, shoving her thick brown hair from her face with the back of her wrist, her hands full with the spray bottle and paper towel. "Cool. Just let me finish here."

I should tell her no one makes Junior Tacone wait.

The thing is—I'm sure she knows that, which is precisely why I find it hot that she gives me so much shit. She knows better. I'm an asshole. I'm dangerous as hell, and she still decides to push me. It's brazen as hell. I love her confidence.

I decide to let it go since my current view makes the wait worth it.

Desiree has this unbelievable body—curves everywhere, but toned muscle underneath. Nice full hourglass figure—big boobs, slender waist, big hips. Sturdy thighs. Like she works out, but can't stop with the Ben & Jerry's. Which is perfect for me. I like a little meat to hold onto. Especially when it's shaped with such delicious mounds.

Right now she's giving me a prime view of her ass, the thin fabric of her scrubs stretched taut across the globes I turned pink just a few hours ago.

"I have a housekeeper, you know."

"Well, she needs to clean the inside of your fridge, Tacone. You tell her that next time."

I pick up a dish towel, spin it into a tight twist and whip it at her ass.

"Ow!" She shrieks and throws her hand back. "Fuck, that hurt." She whirls and seeks my face with her gaze, brows down.

I don't know what my expression shows—probably all the dirty things I want to do to her, because whatever she was going to say next dies on her lips and she flushes like an innocent.

"Come on, sassy-pants. I don't like to wait."

"Of course you don't." She punctuates the words by putting down the spray bottle and towel and shutting the refrigerator door with a little too much force. "Well—you're the boss."

"You seem to keep forgetting it, doll."

I escort her out of the house and to my car, which is sitting in the driveway. She has the audacity to fiddle with my radio on the drive, changing it to some Top 40 station and singing along to the Camila Cabello song *Havana*.

I give her a sidelong glance. With the last name Lopez, I know she's Latina. I'm guessing Puerto Rican, based on the neighborhood where she lives. "You speak Spanish, doll?"

"*Si, jefe.* You speak Italian?"

"*Si.*"

"Lemme hear some. I bet I'll understand it."

"You have a nice voice," I tell her in Italian.

Her full lips stretch into a smile. "*Pues.*"

I like when she blushes because it seems so out of character. Or I guess I just like when *I* make her blush.

We pull into her neighborhood and I find a place to park. She gets out and slams her door. "I sure as hell hope you brought my keys."

"I did." I pull her keyring out of my pocket and twirl it around my forefinger. "And that mouth of yours is going to get you into trouble, doll."

She grins at me, revealing two deep dimples. "You love it and you know it."

I smirk and tuck my hands back in my pockets. "Doesn't mean I won't make you pay for it."

I catch the flash of excitement in her eyes before she turns quickly away and heads up the sidewalk to her building. I follow her at a leisurely pace, enjoying the swing of her delicious ass, the toss of that thick brown hair.

We walk up four flights of stairs to get to her rundown place. It's clean and organized inside—a two bedroom. She heads into one bedroom, I wander over to look in the other. It has a twin bed which hasn't been made up, and a stack of boxes along the wall. I stroll closer to peek at the boxes.

"What are you doing? Stop." She snaps from the doorway of the other bedroom.

I give her a "what?" look.

"Just—get out of there." Her eyes are troubled, mouth set in an unhappy slant.

Hmm. More of her mystery. Who do the boxes belong to? Did someone die? I make a show of shrugging and positioning myself with my back against her front door to wait.

I pull out my phone and shoot a text to Earl Goldfarb, a private investigator we sometimes use for intel. *I need you to research a girl—Desiree Lopez. Lives in Humboldt Park.*

He replies immediately. *Okay. Need me to watch her?*

No. She's with me now. I just want background info on her.

You got it. Priority?

Today. I hit send and shove my phone back in my pocket. I rationalize the intrusion on her privacy as necessary since she's got shit on me now. I need to know her weak spots. But the truth is I want—*need*—to know more about Desiree in general. I need to know everything that makes her tick. What causes her pain. What keeps her up at night. I need into that beautiful head of hers.

Through the open door, I watch her moving swiftly around her room, throwing clothes into a small suitcase.

I'll find out all your secrets, doll. There's nothing you can hide from me.

CHAPTER 5

Desiree

TWO MEN ARRIVE LATE AFTERNOON—MORE Tacones, judging by the resemblance. Junior seems less than enthusiastic to see them and they're subdued as they come into Gio's room, Junior trailing behind them. I wonder if Junior's decision not to take Gio to a hospital was a controversial one.

I'm in the room, repacking the wound, rolling him to another side and changing out the IV bag. "Hi, boys," I breeze, like it's perfectly normal for a nurse to be doing home health care on a gunshot victim.

"This is Desiree," Junior says. "She was Ma's nurse after the hip surgery."

Both men eye me speculatively. "I'm Stefano," the friendlier looking one says with a Hollywood worthy smile. He holds out his hand, but I spread my gloved fingers and shake my head. Not a good time to shake.

"This is Nico," Stefano introduces the other man, who just looks at me coolly. He's as scary as Junior in his own way. All three are handsome as hell, but Junior's definitely the hottest. He's at least ten years older, and I find the age on him attractive. The slight graying at the temples and the hard lines on his face make him look more powerful. Seasoned.

"I heard all about you from your mom. You own the big casino in Vegas, right?" It's where most the Tacone money comes from these days, if I understand correctly.

Stefano nods and they turn their attention to Gio, apparently done with me.

"Hey, Gio. You don't look so hot," Stefano says when Gio's eyes flutter open. He's been mostly out, which is to be expected. I'm keeping him on a healthy dose of pain meds and a mild sedative.

"*Vaffanculo*," Gio mumbles and the two newcomers chuckle. I'm guessing it was some kind of curse.

There's a charged silence in the room.

"Well?" Junior demands. There's a defensive note to his voice and now I'm sure there's conflict over how he handled this. For some reason I feel firmly on his side even though his method involved kidnapping me and making me an accessory to his crimes. It's not super logical, but I guess I don't like seeing him on the defensive. Not when I've seen how much he cares about his wounded brother. I'm sure his decision is costing him in more gray hairs.

"I'm not stupid enough to offer my opinion without you asking for it." Nico's tone is grim.

"Say it," Junior growls.

"I think Gio looks like he's in good hands," Nico says. "But if he takes a turn for the worse, I say take him to the hospital. If the cops come asking, I'll make sure you have the best fucking lawyer in the country there is."

"Just say what? He got skewered roasting marshmallows?" Junior snaps.

I finish with the IV bag, but I'm nosy as hell and want to hear the conversation, so I fiddle with the medications on the dresser.

"You say nothing."

There's a long silence and I turn around because I get the sense they're communicating without words. Sure enough, all eyes are on me.

"Desiree, go downstairs," Junior says. No *please*, no *thank you*. But that's pretty much par for the course with him.

And of course, bluster is par on my course. "Why don't you three go downstairs?" I challenge. "My job is in this room."

Nico and Stefano freeze and I realize I've made a huge mistake. Both shoot glances at Junior as if expecting he's going to explode. Since I'm the one who mouthed off, their fear must be for me. I guess mouthing off when it's just Junior is one thing. Mouthing off in front of others might be cause for correction.

An icy tingle races down my spine, but I toss my hair and raise my brows at Junior, keeping up my bluff.

He reaches for me, and catches my arm, but his grasp isn't rough. He pulls me against his body, my back to his chest. One arm wraps around my waist, one hand cages my throat. Lips at my ear, he murmurs in a voice too low for the others to hear, "Baby, you are definitely getting punished for that."

My pussy clenches at the rumble of sex in his voice.

I don't say anything, but my breath comes in pants.

"Now listen up. We have shit to discuss, and unless you want to be more of an accessory than you already are, you need to get downstairs and out of earshot, *capiche*?"

The hand around my throat isn't tight at all, and his thumb lifts to stroke the side of my jaw—a lover's caress. Our backs are to the others, so it feels like a secret message to me. He's seeking my compliance without losing face.

"Would it kill you to say *please* or *thank you*?" I mutter. I don't know why I'm so stubborn—it's just in my genes, I guess.

I feel his smile against my temple. *"Per favore."* He releases me and I spin around and smirk, far too pleased with myself for getting a concession from this hard man. Of course, he has to go and smack my ass as I head out of the room, settling the score back firmly in his favor.

Pues. Now I know the truth. Junior Tacone gives the girl he's screwing more leeway than his own brothers.

And I kind of love that.

I go downstairs and search Junior's cabinets for something to make for dinner. He has pasta, so I put a pot of water on to boil. I'd unpacked fresh sausages from the groceries Paolo brought earlier—apparently he considers them a staple. I smile to myself at these Italian boys. They fit the stereotype in absolutely every way. It's so cliché it's almost funny.

The men come down about forty minutes later. Stefano wanders into the kitchen while Nico and Junior remain out in the living room, talking.

"We're taking off."

"Yeah? How long are you in town for?"

"We're flying back tonight. Gotta run the business. Listen, you take good care of my brother, okay?"

I stop pushing the sausages around the frying pan and turn to face him. "Gio's going to recover," I promise. I've seen enough of these cases. I mean something could go wrong, but he's got a really great chance of making a full recovery.

"I meant Junior," Stefano corrects and I gape in surprise. He winks at me. "He has a real thing for you," he says. "I haven't seen him like this with a woman before."

I still can't seem to speak, I just stand there with my mouth open, wooden spatula in my hand.

"I hope you'll forgive him for shoehorning you into this."

I swallow.

He shrugs. "Well, it looks like you're already busting his balls on a daily basis, so I probably don't need to worry too much about you, right? You have our *stronzo* brother handled better than any of us."

"What's *stronzo*?"

He grins. "Asshole."

"Stefano, get the fuck away from her," Junior growls from the living room.

His grin widens, and he throws his hands out, Italian

style. "What? I'm not flirting. I'm engaged—you know that. Just giving her a few pointers for handling you." He winks at me again and turns, sauntering out in his thousand dollar suit and shiny dress shoes.

Junior comes into the doorway and gives me a suspicious up and down sweep with his eyes before seeing them to the door. While he's gone, I plate the food for us and set it on the table, then sit down and start eating.

Junior

MADONNA, she cooks.

She cooks, she cleans, she's a better nurse than Florence fucking Nightingale. Where did this woman come from? It's stupid, but the fantasy of keeping her here beyond Gio's recovery flashes through my mind.

Desiree waiting at the door for me in nothing but high heels and her lacy bra and panties, a drink in hand. Desiree on her knees, taking my cock deep while I conduct business on my phone.

It's wrong and fucked up and so damn appealing.

I get a hunk of parmesan from the cheese drawer in the fridge and bring it to the table with the grater.

She grins. "Right. I forgot the cheese."

"What's funny?"

"I just figured there were risks in preparing Italian food for a Sicilian. I knew you'd get me on something."

I grate cheese on both our plates, then open a bottle of

red wine, pour each of us a glass, and sit down. "I'm not getting you on anything." I take a bite and nearly groan with appreciation. She added fresh garlic and maybe some wine to the sauce and it's absolute perfection. "At least not on your cooking."

She meets my gaze, the usual challenge there. "Yeah, well, if you want some scared little bunny who jumps and scurries every time you give an order, she isn't me."

I shovel another bite of food in my mouth. It's so delicious. "We'll talk about it later," I promise. My words have the intended effect. Her nipples poke through the fabric of her bra, tenting the fresh scrubs she put on after we went to her apartment.

Remembering her admonishment earlier, about me not saying please and thank you, I make an effort. The words are rusty on my lips—she's right, I'm out of the habit of using them. "Thank you for cooking, doll. This food is delicious."

She raises her eyebrows. "A compliment from his highness. I can't believe it."

I shake my head. "Keep pushing it, *bambina*. I promise I will make you good and sorry."

Her pupils dilate and she takes a healthy gulp of wine.

"So what's the scoop with your brothers? You guys don't all get along?"

I sigh and reach for my wine, sitting back. "Nah. Not really."

"How many brothers do you have?"

"Four. I'm the oldest. Then Paolo, then Gio. Nico and Stefano are the youngest. I got forced into the mold my father made for me. Stepped into his shoes when he went to prison. Nico and Stefano, they never wanted to be part of the Family business. Nico's smart as fuck. Honestly, he probably would've made the best don out of all of us, but he had no interest. And things don't work that way anyway—it's all about birth order."

I stop and take a long sip of wine. I can't believe I'm telling her all this. It's not like me to make small talk with anyone, and I definitely never spill my guts. And talking about Family? It's forbidden. But she's watching me with such interest, warmth pouring out of those chocolate brown eyes. It's not just easy to talk to her—I *want* to tell her everything.

"Anyway, Nico concocted this plan to take the gambling side of business to Vegas where it's legal. He invested Family money and made a goddamn fortune. That place makes hundreds of millions a year. And it's all legal."

I don't know why I'm gratified that Desiree doesn't seem overly impressed. She doesn't jump in with questions about the casino like most people do when they find out our brother runs the Bellissimo.

"The money comes to all of you, or just him?"

Astute question.

"All of us. Of course, Nico holds a huge percentage of the corporation, but it was Family money that started the business. We all get fat dividends."

"So what business do you run here that gets your brother shot? Nevermind, I know you can't tell me." She dabs her lips with a paper napkin. "But really—couldn't you just retire?"

I shake my head, the familiar ache starting between my

eyes. The one that's there every time I think about Family business. "My father left me to run things. He wants all his business ventures in place when he gets out."

She tilts her head to the side, chewing on a bite of pasta. "I see." After a moment, she says, "Seems like you and Gio and Paolo carry all the risk and Nico and Stefano carry the reward."

Something akin to relief runs through me hearing her say it that way. Sometimes I feel like fucking Cain, jealous of my brother's successes. I'm shackled here, running an outdated, old school business that's dangerous as hell. They're living glamour, money, and sex in Vegas.

And they've made it plain they don't want my help or interference there.

"When does your dad get out?"

"He's got twelve more years on his sentence. He could get out early on good behavior, but I doubt he will. It would be bad press to let a known mobster out."

"Seriously? Twelve years? Your dad has to be what—in his sixties?"

I nod. "Sixty-five."

"So he'll be seventy-seven when he gets out. You really think he's going to still want to run the business? Won't he want to take all those millions and retire in Cabo or something?"

I shake my head. "You don't know my dad. Family business was everything to him. His whole identity. Plus, it's about community service to him. He believes it's our job to still protect the old neighborhoods. To keep the gangs out, keep the innocent pure. It's old-fashioned, but...I don't know." I down my wine and pour another glass. "There's honor in it."

Desiree's face goes soft. "Yeah, I guess there is. You guys are like throwbacks to another time. Warriors who protect your people and keep the order. Your own law."

I rub my eyes when they unexpectedly sting. Upstairs, Gio groans.

Desiree jumps up from the table. "I'll go look in on him."

"I'll clean up," I tell her.

Heaviness descends on me as I pick up the dishes. As I'm cleaning up, a text comes through from Earl.

Call me for the information you requested.

I step outside the front door to call him in case there's anything I don't want Desiree to hear.

"What do you have?"

"Okay, Desiree Lopez. RN at Cook County. Lives on 22nd. You probably already know all that. She's thirty-two. Married at age twenty-six to one Abe Bennett. A low life construction worker and convicted felon. Divorced him last year. The guy is currently wanted for abducting their kid."

"What?"

Merda. I'm gonna kill the bastard.

"Yeah. Five-year-old Jasper Lopez. Last year she was granted full custody on the grounds that her ex was a convicted cocaine dealer and refused to take a urine test to prove he was clean. Two months later, he picked the kid up from preschool and disappeared. That was six months ago.

"Desiree was working for Cook County then, but she

quit to try to find the kid. When her savings ran out, she did some home healthcare work, including for some *schmutz* named Santo Tacone, Junior—you know him? Heh. Anyway, she did that until Cook County hired her back two months ago.

"She's hired the lame-ass private investigator Terry Ryan to find him. Guy's been charging her monthly, and obviously still no kid. Her other bills include student loans from nursing school, her apartment and utilities, cell phone. She has about five grand in credit card debt. That's about it. Doesn't look like she has any hobbies other than work, finding her kid, and Zumba classes that are free through the hospital wellness plan."

Desiree. Knowing the source of her struggle—and I knew there had to be one because she's too smart and talented to have such a shit life—makes me root for her even more.

"I want you to find the boy."

"Jasper?"

"Yeah. Put every resource you have on it. Hire other P.I.s—I'll pay for it. Find her *stronzo* ex. *Capiche?*"

"You got it. Can I talk to Desiree to get more information?"

"No. Just find the kid."

"Oh yeah, it's that easy. I'll just magically produce him."

"You telling me you can't handle this job?" I snap. I might let Desiree give me shit. I sure as hell don't let private dicks speak with disrespect.

"No, no, no. Don't get your feathers ruffled. I'll find the kid."

"Watch the attitude, Earl. And I want regular updates."

"You'll get them."

"Good." I end the call but I don't go back inside. Not until I'm sure I won't look at Desiree with sympathy—which I know she'd hate.

Cristo. She shouldn't have to suffer like this. To have her own child ripped from her.

Well, fuck. I know something about that, don't I? The ache from Mia's death rips through my chest.

But her child is still alive, and I'm sure as hell going to make sure she gets him back.

CHAPTER 6

Desiree

I GET Gio settled with more pain meds.

Maybe I'm being a chicken, but I don't want to go back downstairs yet. Talking to Junior—really *talking* tonight makes him all too likeable.

And I already can't handle my over-the-top attraction to the guy. I sure as hell don't need to fall in love here.

Junior Tacone's not the kind of guy I want to be in a relationship with. Even though he's nothing like my ex, I've had my fill of men who run on the illegal side of things. If I ever get into another relationship it's going to be with a nice, normal guy. An accountant or salesman. Someone who's respectable and friendly. The kind of guy you could bring to any party.

Not a scary-ass mafioso.

A sexy-as-hell warrior who carries the weight of his

entire family on his shoulders. Who takes very sweet care of his mother. And seems capable of getting things—any sort of thing—done. A smart, ruthless man who does what he believes he needs to do without apology.

Crap, I'm totally falling for Junior Tacone.

And that's just plain stupid.

I switch on the television in Gio's room and very gingerly climb onto the bed. I don't want to jostle Gio—he's in enough discomfort as it is.

Junior doesn't come upstairs. Maybe he feels the need to pull back, too.

Or maybe there's nothing to pull back from.

No, that's bullshit. He's into me. He's been into me since we first met. And we've already had sex.

Holy shit—what was I thinking? I can't believe I had sex with Junior Tacone. This morning seems so long ago. But when I remember how blistering hot it was, my body flushes with the desire for more.

I want Tacone's authoritative hands controlling my body again. Want him talking dirty, making all my fantasies come true as he pretends to take me against my will. I think of the way he pulled me against him when his brothers were here, the soft growl of his warning voice right against my ear.

I make it through a couple TV shows, but my mind is on sex. It's on Junior's threat to punish me again.

Did he forget? Is he waiting for something?

Maybe I need to go downstairs to get his attention.

I'm tempted to leave the TV on so Gio can't hear if I make noise but then I wouldn't be able to hear him if he needs anything. He's too out of it to hear anything, anyway.

I brush my teeth and pad down the stairs.

I hear Junior on the phone. He's not in the living room or the kitchen. I peek around behind the staircase and see a light on in what must be his office. He's sitting behind a desk, a glass of scotch in his hand as he speaks into the phone.

He catches sight of me and stops, gesturing with his tumbler, eyes boring a hole right through me.

Oh lordy. He hasn't forgotten. I definitely see dark promise brimming in the depths of those chocolate browns.

I spin on my heel, like a scared rabbit and beeline it for the kitchen. Turns out Junior's offer to clean up wasn't legit. He put our dishes in the dishwasher but the pots and pans are still on the stove and nothing's been wiped down.

I'd be annoyed except it's not my kitchen and not my job, so I don't have to clean it.

But I'm totally going to because it gives me something to do. I wash the pots and spray and wipe the table, then the countertops.

Junior's voice goes silent and I hear his soft tread as he comes down the hall and into the kitchen. My heart rate picks up. I don't turn around even though I know he's standing in the doorway.

Probably looking at my ass.

He comes closer.

I still don't acknowledge his presence.

"You've been cleaning the same spot for forty seconds

now." His baritone rolls through my body like dark sunshine.

"You're counting?" My voice sounds husky and foreign. I stop and toss the balled up paper towel into the garbage, still not turning around. "I thought you were supposed to clean up."

"There you go again, running that mouth." He cages me against the counter, my back to him. His teeth sink into my shoulder.

My knees nearly buckle. He grasps both my wrists and pins them to the counter, moving at a leisurely pace. My breath catches. Anticipation buzzes. He reaches past me and pulls a wooden spoon out of the canister.

When he smacks me with it, I yelp. It's way sexier as a thought than a reality. It freaking hurts.

He's going fast, whacking my ass right and left and I immediately fight him, trying to scoot out of the way.

"Ow—whoa!" My brain spins around how to stop it. "Peanut butter."

The spoon immediately clatters on the counter in front of me. "Okay, no spoon. But you don't get to safe word out of taking my cock."

My brain stutters on that for just a moment—because, yeah—I do. But I decide he's just dirty talking and I definitely don't want him to stop. Not when I'm already soaking my panties.

He cups my ass and squeezes roughly. It diminishes the sting of the spanking he just gave me. I push back into his touch. He pops my ass with the flat of his hand. It feels delicious. So much better than the damn spoon.

"Okay, doll. I know you're terrible at following orders,

but I'm giving you one now. You have three seconds for those panties to hit the floor or I pick that wooden spoon back up."

"You can't—"

"One."

Crazy fucking Italian. I yank my scrubs and panties down, kicking out of my shoes at the same time.

"Two."

"I said *peanut butter* to the spoon," I complain as I hop on one foot to get out of the leg of my scrubs.

Junior's rolling up his sleeves with a stern daddy look as he watches me. "Three."

I kick off the other leg and the panties go flying with the scrubs. I point. "Panties are on the floor. See?"

I love the ghost of a smile dancing over his lips. *"Brava ragazza."* He steps in and pulls my scrub top over my head.

I get a deep whiff of his masculine scent—soap and a trace of cologne. "What's that mean?"

"Good girl." He reaches behind me to unsnap my bra. I'm totally naked now and he's fully dressed. It's hot as hell.

"You training me?" Ms. Bluster has to keep pushing.

He wraps my bra around my neck and turns me around, holding it snug against my throat like he's going to choke me with it. My hand flies to the fabric and my body registers the threat with a rush of endorphins. My pussy registers it all as miraculous foreplay. "You think you're tamable, doll?" He tugs on the bra, just enough to make me nervous. "I'm not sure you are."

He releases it, just as abruptly as he used it as a weapon. It falls to the floor, a harmless undergarment once more. "Hands on the counter, baby. Stick your ass out for me." Once more he reaches past me. I think he's going for another implement in the bin, but instead he grabs the bottle of olive oil. When he drips some down my crack, I shake my head. "Nuh uh. No way."

He covers my mouth so I can't say my safe word. "No, baby. You disrespect me in front of my brothers, you're going to take it in the ass. Even if it's just my finger."

Just his finger.

Shit!

Okay, I can handle this. Right?

Lord, I'm all fluttery and hot. My arousal drips onto my inner thighs. Junior rubs a digit over my anus, circling and massaging it.

It shouldn't feel so good, but it does. Erotic, pleasurable. *Wrong.*

But so right.

He works his finger—or maybe thumb—into my ass. I breathe deep and force myself to relax the tight ring of muscles, to let him in. It's not painful, but it's horribly embarrassing. It's humiliating pleasure. Each time he pumps his finger, my pussy grows wetter.

I start moaning. My legs tremble. He keeps at it, thoroughly finger-fucking my ass. Showing me he owns me. He holds his finger in deep and slaps the lower part of my ass where it meets the thigh. He spanks me again and again, all the while twisting his finger around in my ass.

"Ung," I groan.

"Reach down between your legs and feel how wet that made you."

I was dying to touch myself, actually. I comply immediately and find my sex swollen and dripping wet. My fingers sink into my pussy without me even meaning to dip them in. He eases his finger out of my anus and shifts to the right of me to wash his hands in the sink.

I work my fingers between my legs because my pussy's dying for some attention. The tissues are swollen and slick, flooded with my arousal.

Junior returns seconds later, his fingers pushing over mine, rubbing my throbbing clit. "You love having your ass fucked, don't you, doll?"

All I can do is moan. I'm all hot and needy now. My pussy aches to be filled by him.

"Don't you?" He slaps my ass.

I want to say no. I really do. I'm still totally scared of butt sex. But damn if I don't whisper the truth. "Yes."

"Disrespect me in front of others again and you're gonna get my cock in your ass." He bites my ear. "*Capiche?*" He whispers the word, his hot breath feathering over my ear.

My pussy clenches and he feels it, rubs my clit harder. "*Capito*," I murmur.

"Good girl." He holds my hips and crouches down, lifting one of my knees up toward the counter top and licking into me.

"Oh fuck, Junior."

I didn't even know it was possible to be eaten out from behind.

Oh, but it is. And Junior Tacone definitely knows what he's doing. He licks and sucks and nips. Penetrates me with his stiffened tongue. Penetrates with his fingers while he licks and sucks and nips.

The room fills with the sound of my cries—quiet sex is still not part of my repertoire.

He smacks his lips. "You taste so good, baby."

"Junior." My voice is a whine because I really want to come.

He stands up. I turn around, needing to be fucked. Needing to offer myself up. But he shakes his head. "Face the counter." His lips are glossy with my juices, his voice sounds three octaves lower than usual. He pulls a condom out of his pocket and rips it out. "*Now*, baby."

I drag my lower lip through my teeth as I turn around and brace my hands on the counter.

He lifts my knee up like he had it when he ate me out and pushes into me. One hard thrust and he's buried deep.

I cry out, close my eyes in pleasure. He commands my body—one hand firmly holding up my thigh, the other braced on the counter so I'm caged between his arms and pounds into me.

My eyes roll back in my head and a stream of gibberish flows out of my mouth—some English, some Spanish. Hell, I don't know, I probably even try to speak Italian for him.

His breath grows rough. His grip tightens on my leg.

"Yes, Junior, please," I plead, because I'm close—so close—and I can tell he is too. His thrusts grow erratic and then he slams so hard I'm unable to hold myself away from the edge of the counter. I hit it and give a little squeal of pain.

"Sorry!" Junior pants, pulling out and spinning me around. He cups my chin and peers down in my face. "You all right?"

"Don't stop," I beg, even though he already has.

He picks me up by the waist and sits my bare ass on the counter, then spreads my knees wide and licks into me again. I clutch at his head as he licks with fervor. I tear at his hair, screaming loud enough to wake every neighbor.

He pauses, lifting his eyes to me. "You don't come," he warns, employing his stern don voice. He flicks his tongue over my clit. "You don't ever come until I give you permission. Got it?"

I nod quickly, eager to do whatever it takes to climax.

He scoops me off the counter and I wrap my legs around his waist. He carries me into the living room where he drops me and bends me over the stuffed arm of his couch.

"I need you where I can pound you hard like you deserve," he explains.

The position is actually perfect—the padded arm of the sofa cushions my hips and the height and angle are perfect. The moment he enters me, I'm ready to come. Every thrust sets me on fire. My inner thighs tremble and quake, my voice warbles in my throat.

And then he shoves his thumb back up my ass.

The sensation of having both holes filled at once sets off fireworks behind my eyes. Junior pounds into me, holding me captive with his thumb, owning me again. "You gonna be a good girl now? Huh, doll? Gonna keep sassing me every chance you can get?"

"Yes...no!" I can't figure out the right words to say to get my reward. I'm so desperate to come, I'd say anything. "Junior, God, please."

He curses and slams in hard, slapping my ass with his loins four more times before he shouts.

I don't come. Maybe because the thumb in my ass keeps me open—like my body won't contract around it. I don't know how he knows it, but he pulls his thumb out, reaches around the front of my hips and rubs my clit. "Come, Desiree."

That's all it takes. I go off like a rocket ship, my whole body convulsing as I squeeze the cum out of his cock.

The room spins.

~

Junior

"How did you know?" Desiree croaks.

For one bizarre moment, I think she means about her missing son. "Know what, doll?"

"That I hadn't come?"

I chuckle. "Baby, you never stopped begging." The woman is off the charts with her sex noise. I mean, she coulda been a porn star. I've never had a woman show so much appreciation in my life.

"I didn't?"

"I thought you were being especially obedient because I told you not to come." I pull out, lift her up and turn her around. She falls back to sit on the end of the sofa, like she's too trembly to stand. "Were you having a hard time reaching the finish line?"

I don't know why I'm speaking in metaphor when I've already said every filthy thing on the planet to her.

She shoves her thick hair back from her flushed face. "Yeah. It was hard with something in my ass."

I cock my head. Again, maybe I misread her. I thought for sure she enjoyed the ass play. "Because it hurt?"

She laughs, leaning her forehead against my chest like she needs to hide her face for this conversation. "No, it just was different, that's all. I didn't want to tighten up when I was being held open."

I chuckle again and stroke the back of her neck.

After a minute, when our breath has slowed, she lifts her head. "You'd better disinfect the hell out of that counter. I can't believe you put my bare ass on it."

A surprised laugh comes out of me. "I promise I will bleach the fuck out of it. And yes, it was my job to clean up tonight, but I got sidetracked with a phone call. I'm sorry, I didn't mean to leave the mess for you."

If anyone who knows me was present, they would shoot me and asked what I've done with the real Junior Tacone, because I never apologize. It's a trait my father taught me. Although maybe he's also the guy who taught me that none of those rules apply to the woman in your life.

Even not knowing me, Desiree appears surprised. "I was just giving you shit. If I didn't feel like doing the dishes, I would've just left them for you to do in the morning."

I smile. I'm glad she knows I don't expect her to cook and clean for me. The fact that she does it anyway does strange things to my chest. "Good."

But reality settles back in. Desiree is a mother. She has a five-year-old son I'm going to make sure gets home with her. She's not going to stick around cooking and cleaning for me. She's not going to want to bring that boy of hers anywhere near me.

And that's how it should be.

I'm dangerous. I bring darkness and hatred to everyone around me, myself included.

The last thing Desiree Lopez needs is to get dragged down by someone like me.

CHAPTER 7

Desiree

"Listen, doll." Junior cups my chin in that stern way of his. "I'll run out and get us coffee if you promise not to make a break for it. Are we past that now?"

"Can I see my phone again?"

He let me check texts and messages last night—with him looking over my shoulder the whole time, of course. There was a reply from my mom, but nothing else. No word from the private investigator or work.

"I don't know why you think this is negotiation. What you're getting out of the deal is hot coffee and maybe a pastry. I'm asking if you're gonna stay put or if I need to tie you to the bed. Because, baby, I will. And we both know you'd like it." His voice deepens on the last words and I feel the vibration everywhere.

He's so right. Heat floods my nether regions at his words. Still, I keep making demands. "Just let me see it."

He sticks his hand in his pocket and produces my phone. "You don't have any messages." He swipes across the screen and opens my texts to show me. "Oh wait, you do have a new one."

He shows me the screen. My co-worker and friend Lucy texted. "You're sick?"

"Can I answer? Tell her the same thing I told my mom? She's a good friend."

He nods and watches me closely as I type a response, like he's looking for some sign I wanted my phone for some other reason.

I didn't. I'm not going to call for help or try to escape. I may have been coerced, but now we made our bargain. I'm sticking to it.

I called in sick, but I actually have a home healthcare job that pays double this week. Don't tell anyone! Then I put in three emojis of money bags. She knows how badly I need the money and will totally support me on this decision.

Even though it wasn't really *my* decision.

When I'm finished, I hand the phone back. "I'll take a latte and an egg sandwich, if they have them. Where are you going?"

"Starbucks. Ham and cheese?"

"Yes, please."

"You gonna stay?" He puts that note of warning in his voice that makes my panties wet.

I give him a shove toward the door. "Of course I'll stay. I need my coffee. Make it a large, *capiche*?"

His deep chuckle sends frissons of pleasure through my body.

I like making him laugh. Way too much. I need to guard my heart against this man because he is worming in far too quickly.

"Listen, I'm not gonna call a bodyguard because I'll be right back, but keep the door locked and don't answer it for anyone."

A chill slithers through me, but I nod.

He leaves and I head back upstairs to clean and dress Gio's wounds and check his vitals.

When the doorbell rings, I freeze.

Okay, I'm not supposed to answer it. Should I call Junior?

It rings again, several times, fast. Like it's someone who knows Junior well. Definitely not a door-to-door salesman.

"Junior?" A woman's voice calls out.

A wave of cold washes over me. There's a woman? Of course there's a woman. He's a filthy rich, powerful man. He probably has a whole handful of women hanging around him at all times.

My empty stomach turns.

She rings again, several times fast.

Ugh. I'm seriously going to be sick. I stand on the landing, staring down the stairs at the front door. Like I can will the little tramp away with my laser vision.

A key turns in the lock. Oh my God. Who is this? She has a key?

This isn't some floozy. It's a serious girlfriend.

The door swings open and a very pretty, very young

woman steps in. "Junior?" She looks up the stairs, her eyes widening when she sees me.

"Oh shit," she says, and comes flying up the stairs at me.

I freeze, my gut tighter than a drum. Is she some psycho girlfriend coming to attack me? But she pushes past me like I don't exist, and steps into Gio's room.

"Gio!" she cries out, fear in her voice. "Oh my God, what happened?" Now she whirls to look at me again. "Where's Junior?"

"Who the hell are you?" I demand, even though I probably have the least right to make demands. No, fuck that. He slept with me. I can demand all I want.

The sound of the front door opening comes from downstairs. The woman doesn't wait for me to answer, but charges out on the landing. "Junior, what the fuck?"

I charge out onto the landing, too, and do my best to kill him with a glare. He lets out a stream of angry Italian, sets the drink tray and Starbucks bag down on an end table and marches up the stairs, looking grim.

Ex-girlfriend, then. She must be an ex-girlfriend, because he doesn't look guilty, he looks pissed. "What the fuck are you doing here?"

"What in the hell happened to Gio?" she counters, and waves a hand at me. "And who is this? I can't believe you dragged some random nurse into this."

"How did you get in?" He looks past her at me. "Did you let her in?"

She's definitely not welcome. The jealous twist below my ribs starts to ease. "She had a key." I look at her more closely, and then it dawns on me with a hit of warm relief. "Alessia." Junior's little sister. I saw her in photographs when I took care of her mom, but she was away at college. She graduated in December, I think. Or she was supposed to.

She turns a surprised look at me.

"Desiree nursed Ma after her surgery," Junior explains, as if I'm the biggest question in the room.

Alessia points at Gio. "When were you going to tell us?"

Junior's eyes narrow. "Never. Why in the hell are you here?"

"Stefano and Nico stopped by yesterday. And Ma got worried because you haven't been by, and she knew they were out here for some reason. Plus Paolo's acting weird and Gio won't answer his phone." She waves a hand at Gio. *"Obviously."*

Junior runs a hand through his hair, rumpling it. "So Ma sent you?"

"Well, I said I would find out." Her eyes abruptly brim with tears. "Jesus, Junior, what the fuck? Is he going to be okay?"

"Yes," Junior and I both answer at the same time. I don't know why I feel like I need to back Junior up with his family. He's the kingpin, after all. But they all act like he's the bad guy, and it bugs the hell out of me.

She looks at me searchingly. I guess it makes sense—I'm the one dressed like a nurse. "The bullet went clean through," I tell her. "No apparent damage to organs, not too much blood loss. The wounds will heal on their own with time and rest. He's on painkillers, antibiotics and sedation, so he's comfortable. There's no reason to believe he won't make a full recovery."

A couple tears fall down her cheeks and she nods. "I won't ask what happened," she mumbled.

"Good," Junior says. "And I don't want you telling Ma, either."

She throws her hands into the air. "I'm not going to lie! She knows something's up, Junior. You'd better figure out what to tell her yourself, but don't ask me to lie for you."

"See, that's why you shouldn't be here, Lessa. And why do you have a fucking key to my place?"

"You had me house sit last year when you went to the Old Country, remember?"

"Oh yeah."

She slides a glance at me. "Why is it okay for her to be here, but not your own sister?"

Junior gives her a withering look. "Are you a fucking nurse?"

"You know what I mean."

Junior shakes his head. "Don't ask me about business. You know better."

She rolls her eyes. "You sound just like Pops."

"And that's exactly why I shouldn't have to tell you this shit. Go home. Tell Ma everything's fine. I'll come see her next week. Don't come back here without an invitation."

Alessia shakes her head. "You're such an ass, Junior."

I bite my lips to keep from giving her a piece of my mind.

She turns and walks down the stairs, and Junior and I both follow. At the front door, she turns and offers her cheeks to Junior, who kisses both of them, like they weren't just yelling at each other. Something about it warms my heart.

This family's not that different from mine. From anyone's. They have their squabbles and problems. But they love and care for each other just like the rest of us.

Junior mutters something in Italian. I can't figure out the translation, but it seems like a normal goodbye thing.

"*Grazie*," she answers. "Nice to meet you," she says to me.

"Tell your mom I said hi," I say, because I'm not feeling as warm and fuzzy toward her as I am toward her mom. "Or—I guess don't—since you're not telling her what's going on," I babble.

She gives a wave as Junior practically pushes her out the door.

"You are not the popular brother this week, are you?" I say when she's gone, to lighten the mood.

"I consistently win most hated," he says grimly. His face is back to the closed mask he usually wears, and it kinda breaks my heart to think that his family hates him. He pulls one of the coffee cups from the carrier and hands it to me.

"Well, you're still the apple of your mama's eye," I say, which is true. The woman practically lit up every time he came to visit. Not that she didn't speak proudly about all her children. I take a sip and moan with pleasure.

Junior goes still, gaze fixed on my lips.

I enjoyed the show. That's what he'd said the first night about watching me eat ice cream. My lady parts start tingling. Knowing I turn this powerful man on with a simple act of sipping coffee or eating ice cream gives me a huge boost of confidence.

I hold his gaze as I take another sip. This time I'm conscious of the moan of approval I give it. "This hits the spot," I murmur. "Thank you."

"You probably enjoyed watching me get my balls busted by the little princess, didn't you?"

"Actually, I wanted to throw her out," I answer honestly.

His face warms, the harsh lines relaxing into fondness. He shakes his head. "You're something else, doll."

"Yeah, except when she walked in here with her key, I didn't just want your balls busted, I wanted them cut off."

He chokes on his coffee.

"I thought you had some girlfriend you hadn't told me about." I cock a hip. "Are there other women, Tacone?"

He flashes a cocky grin. "Oh, now it's Tacone, huh? No, baby. No girlfriends." Then his smile fades. "I guess I should tell you I never officially divorced my ex-wife. We've been separated for ten years, though."

I blink at him. "Why not?"

He shrugs and I watch his face closely. He hands me the Starbucks bag. "Here's your sandwich."

I grab it, narrowing my gaze. "No, really, Junior. Why didn't you get divorced?"

"She didn't want to be with me anymore, so I let her go. But she suffers from depression. She can't work. She's still my responsibility."

A bitter taste fills my mouth. Lord, if I felt jealous of the imagined girlfriend, it's nothing compared to how I feel knowing he still financially supports his ex-wife. Well, still his wife, technically.

I know it relates to my own issues with money and men. Abe always spent our money. Never contributed to the household. And of course, since he's been gone, since he took Jasper, I've been living on nothing, with all my money still paying off the divorce lawyer I had to hire to win custody and now the private investigator.

So the idea of some woman giving up Junior and playing too damaged to work so he'll keep supporting her? It just twists like a knife in my chest. And then another thought occurs to me.

Maybe this was the situation he chose so he could sleep with whoever he wanted, but she had to stay tied to him forever. It seems like a kind of jealous *mafioso* man thing to do. I tilt my head to the side. "So does she sleep with other men?"

Disgust crosses his face. "Fuck no. I seriously doubt it. She'd better not."

The knife twists deeper. "She better not? You are seriously an asshole, Junior."

"Yeah?" He looks slightly pissed, slightly confused.

"I get it. You want to have all the ass you want, all your freedom, but keep her locked up as Mrs. Tacone for the rest of her life. Real decent of you."

His lip curls. "You don't know what the hell you're talking about. It's not like that. Not at all."

I fold my arms across my chest. "Really? Well then explain it to me."

His lips tighten. His eyes have gone dead. It's definitely scary Junior looking back at me. We blink at each other for a minute, and then he gestures toward the kitchen. "Go eat your fucking breakfast."

"Right," I say, my hand tightening on the food. "You just put me in my place, didn't you?" I turn and march into the kitchen, not waiting for his reaction.

This time, I'm definitely sure he's not turned on by my defiance.

There won't be any punishment sex for this one.

Not that I'd welcome it.

No, I just called him out on his shit, and he didn't want to hear it.

But it's good. Now I know what kind of man he is. Not that I didn't already. I just got lulled into thinking there might be more to him, underneath the frightening exterior.

But there's not.

This is the kind of man who consumes people. And if I get stuck in his web, I'll get consumed, too. If he decides I belong to him, he'll keep me prisoner forever.

~

Junior

I THROW BACK another scotch and sigh.

I have everyone out on the street looking for Vlad, but the Russians have gone totally underground. No one knows where to find the guy. I should be satisfied that he's gone into hiding, but I'm not. Because he's probably plotting revenge. Which means I need to find him and kill him before he finds me.

Upstairs, I hear the television turn off. I gave Desiree a wide berth all day, and she was all business with me.

I don't know why I didn't think my marital status would be a deal-breaker for Desiree, but I didn't. Fuck, if I had any idea her reaction would be so negative, I never would have told her.

No, that's not true.

It would've been worse if she heard it from one of my brothers, and *Madonna*, I know one of them would've been happy to throw that at her just to screw me.

But her implication that Marne is a kept woman—like I won't divorce her because I don't want to let her go is way off base.

I would've loved for her to go on with her life. Meet some other asshole to take care of her. Relieve me of the guilt and fucking shadow that's always hanging over me. What we could've been without our tragedy. The happy, nuclear family.

Aw, *merda*. Maybe that's not true. It's possible Desiree's right. I'm a possessive asshole and I didn't want her to be out in the world without me.

No. No. I don't think that's true. If she'd been respectful, if she'd gotten her life together—got a job. Maybe some good counseling. If she came to me and said she'd fallen in love with some other guy, I would've kissed her cheeks and told her I was happy for her. I swear to Christ.

I mean, she coulda filed for divorce. I never told her she had to stay married to me. Hell, she could've divorced me and taken half of everything I own. It's not like she has to stay tethered to me to keep food on her table. She'd probably actually be living larger if she divorced me.

But maybe she's too afraid of me.

I never hurt her—never even slapped her ass, but she was always a little skittish. She knows what I am. And she also thinks I blame her for Mia.

Maybe I do, I don't know. The darkness in that house consumed the both of us after our little girl's death.

All I know is that I carry the weight of all of it, right in the center of my chest. Guilt for not knowing how to deal with my own grief. Not being able to help Marne with hers. Guilt for not wanting to be with her anymore. Not wanting to live in that house with all the reminders.

What I had with Desiree—it's over now, I know that. It was like a retractable ceiling opening up on my life. Sunlight pouring down and warming me, even with all the usual shit shows, like worry over Gio and my siblings' wrath over the way I handled it.

But that ceiling's closed. There's no untangling me from the dark web that is my life. The one my father created for me and I wove even tighter around myself. I'll never be free of Marne, or my responsibilities of running *La Famiglia*. Or the wounds I inflicted on all those around me by always playing the asshole.

There's no point in even thinking about what might be different—what might be possible if I divorce Marne, because Desiree's already smartened up.

She knows better than to give any part of herself to me.

Because I'll take it.

Consume her.

And God knows, I would never, ever let her get away.

That's why she was so offended about me not getting divorced. It's not because she's pissed I fooled around with her when I'm not available, although there might have been a little of that. No, it's because she recognized the dark truth of the matter. She could just as easily end up on my leash. And it's nowhere she ever wants to be.

CHAPTER 8

Desiree

I DREAM Jasper's in his bed crying for me. I try to comfort him, but he can't feel my arms, doesn't hear my words. I'm a ghost to him.

I wake up to the sound of Gio's groan. I remember it's Jasper's birthday before I even open my eyes. It's been four days since Junior kidnapped me and brought me here to take care of Gio. It feels like months. And I just want to be home right now, where I could cry into my pillow all day without seeing anyone.

Of course, I knew this day was coming. I knew it like a countdown to a massive breakdown for me. Weight crushes my chest. I feel two hundred years old as I ease out of bed.

I check Gio's vitals and add more painkiller to his IV before I head to the shower.

The tears start while I'm in there and they just don't stop. Not like full-on sobbing, more like a steady drip. A leaky faucet that won't turn off.

Dammit.

I get out of the shower, dry off and get dressed in my Dickie scrubs—red today.

The tears just keep on running.

They drip the whole time I clean Gio's wounds and put fresh bandages on.

"Hey." Junior's standing in the doorway, holding my phone. He catches sight of the tears before I quickly brush them away. "You okay?"

"Yep," I say with determination. Like I'm going to somehow make it true.

"What happened?"

"Nothing. I don't want to talk about it."

I grab my phone out of his hand, since I'm assuming he's bringing it because I got a message. He still refuses to let me have it or use it without him watching my every move, but at least he checks my messages frequently and shows me as soon as something comes in.

"Text from your mom," he tells me.

Fresh tears start because I already feel her sympathy, her support, her love. My mom is so connected to me and my emotions, it's sometimes scary.

Sending you energy and healing light on this difficult day.

I snort-choke back a sob. Coming from my mom, that's a real promise. In addition to nursing at the hospital, she also volunteers as an energy healer, going around giving reiki treatments to anyone who wants it. And she's a powerful healer. Sometimes I swear she's the one who saves the most lives at that place.

"Why is today difficult?" Junior asks.

"None of your business," I snap, thrusting the phone back at him after sending my mom a heart emoji. "Let's move him." Every eight hours we roll Gio from his side, to his back, to his other side. Even though I could probably do it on my own, I get Junior to help, because Gio's such a big guy.

We roll him over and he wakes and uses the bed pan, cursing in Italian the whole time. Junior answers in Italian, using calm, reassuring tones and Gio settles and closes his eyes once more.

"We should get you out of the house." Junior's looking at me like I'm going to crack. "You're probably sick of being cooped up here. You definitely deserve a break. I'll get Paolo to come stay with Gio, and I'll take you anywhere that sounds good."

My lips tremble. I seriously can't take Junior being nice right now.

I would much rather have him be an asshole so I can get prickly and keep my shit together.

"Or Paolo can take you out, if you need a break from me." He takes a step back and shoves his hands in his pockets.

My lip curls. "I'm not going anywhere with Paolo."

Junior pulls out his phone and starts thumbing over the screen. "Where do you want to go?"

I shrug. "I'm really not in the mood, Junior."

"No shit, doll. I'm not asking you on a date. I'm trying

to figure out what would be...I don't know, *nourishing* to you." He makes a big gesture with his hands as he talks.

"Nourishing?"

"Nurturing—whatever the fuck the word is. What do you do to make yourself feel better? Go see a movie? How about exercise? I'll take you to my gym up the street. You can take yoga or Zumba or whatever."

I perk up a tiny bit over Zumba and he catches it. The Latin cardio dance class is my favorite form of exercise.

"You like that idea?" He scrolls on his phone. "There's Zumba at 11:00 a.m." I don't know how he knew I wanted Zumba and not yoga. The man's a mind reader.

It's hard to imagine I could muster the energy to do a cardio class right now, though. "I don't know," I say.

He points at me, the scary-stern face on. "You're going to Zumba. And what else? You like shopping? A little retail therapy?"

I snort. "Yeah right. With what money?"

"You can spend my money. That'll be fun, no?" He tips his head to catch my eye.

A reluctant smile tugs at my lips. "Could be," I admit.

Damn my turn-on with men spending money on me.

Damn Junior for showing up like a white knight when I'm at my weakest.

"Come on, I'll take you to breakfast."

Oh shit. Now it does feel like a date. And he's spending money on me. Taking care of me.

It scares me how much I want to be taken care of. Especially by a wealthy, powerful man like Junior.

But that's exactly why I need to keep the barriers up

around my heart. Because I already fear I won't be walking out of here with it intact.

"Should I change?" I ask dubiously, looking down at my scrubs.

He shrugs. "Not for me. Wear whatever makes you feel good, doll."

Yeah, not scrubs. Scrubs are the world's ugliest uniform ever. I grab a pair of jeans and fitted long-sleeved shirt and take them into the bathroom to change.

Not that Junior hasn't already seen all of me.

But Gio hasn't, and I don't want him getting an eyeful if he comes back around.

Junior's still on his phone when I come back out, but when he looks up, his eyes bug out a little. The emerald green shirt is sexy—I brought it on purpose to torture Junior. It hugs my breasts and opens in a V to show a little cleavage. The jeans are flattering too—they're tight and hug my ass, but the denim has a little stretch to it, so they're ultra-comfortable. I pull on a pair of boots and fluff my still-wet hair.

"Damn," Junior says.

"What?"

He just shakes his head and mutters, "And I thought you were hot in scrubs."

Okay, I might be starting to feel a little better, even though the heaviness still pushes at my chest.

I pack some gym clothes and we head down the stairs. "When is Paolo coming?" I ask.

"He'll be here in time for Zumba. Gio will be all right for an hour while we go to breakfast."

"You're speaking with all your medical expertise?" I

can't help giving him a hard time. It's like it's a job I was born to do.

"I'd slap your ass, but I have a feeling today would be the day you'd deck me for it."

I'm getting closer to smiling.

~

Junior

I FORCE myself to work out at the gym, because *Dio*, if I watch Desiree shaking those hips in her yoga pants and tank during Zumba, I'm going to march in there, throw her over my shoulder and carry her to the locker room shower. And let me tell you, I wouldn't be washing her hair in that shower.

I text Earl to find out the significance of the day for Desiree.

He replies right away—*it's the boy's birthday.*

Well, fuck.

I know how hard those dates are. Except my child is dead. And Desiree's isn't, he's been stolen from her. I fire off another text to Earl putting more pressure on him to find her son. *Hire every detective in town. Get them all on the case,* I tell him. *I want this kid found yesterday.*

Cheering people up isn't my strong suit, as evidenced by my wife's mental state following Mia's death.

I wait for her outside her class. Fuck if it isn't still going and I do get an eyeful of those hips lighting the room on fire. The class runs over and I can't move because I don't want to miss a single second of it.

It's worse knowing what she likes, because I start imagining forcing her to have sex in a thousand dirty ways. But she doesn't want that.

Not anymore.

And the fantasy's only hot if she's actually into it.

The five minutes feel like fifty, but finally the class ends and she walks out, a towel around her neck. I don't dare look at the way her breasts stretch that tank top or I'll sprout a chub that everyone will see.

"I'm gonna take a quick shower," she tells me. "Meet you outside the locker room."

I nod and watch her ass as she walks away. She's not strutting—I still see the defeat in her posture—but she has all the right junk in the trunk.

Desiree is the full package. Smart, sassy, hot as hell. I wonder what went wrong with her marriage. The guy has to be a douche not to do everything he could to keep her.

Well, obviously he's more than a douche. He's a *testa di cazzo*. He stole their kid from her.

I shower and change and meet her outside the locker room. Her hair's still wet, like she rushed to get out and meet me. It's fucking freezing outside.

"Get back in there and dry your hair," I tell her. "You'll fucking freeze."

She rolls her eyes. "I'll be fine."

I block her path. "Hey," I make my voice sharp, like I'm coming down on one of my soldiers for disrespect.

She jerks a little, then slaps my chest. "Jesus, you are

such an asshole. Do you seriously have to bully me every second of the day?"

I might feel bad, considering she's having a shit day, but it's good to see the spark back in her. I give her a hard stare until she rolls her eyes and turns around with a huff, marching back to the locker room.

When she comes back out, her hair is a dark, glossy curtain over her shoulders, framing her lovely face. She always has it back in a ponytail, so I'm momentarily struck by her model-worthy beauty.

I look at my phone. "No messages from Paolo. I'm taking you shopping."

She doesn't want to like it, but I can tell she does. I know she's been scraping by. A woman like her deserves to be spoiled.

We're not close to any big malls, but I take her to an area of my suburb with the fancy shops and find a spot to park on the street. I should probably call in one of the guys to stand as bodyguard, because Vlad could be anywhere, but I don't think I've been followed, and I don't see anything suspicious.

"You have three thousand dollars to spend in fifty minutes. You don't get to keep any money you don't spend, and everything you buy has to be for yourself."

She stops and turns rounded eyes on me, lips parting.

I want to kiss them.

Fuck.

What's wrong with me?

It's one thing to want to fuck a girl. But kissing? I haven't kissed a woman since Marne. Not one.

I don't know—it's too intimate. Or too emotional. It's just not something I ever want to do.

But yeah, I want to kiss her. Right fucking now.

"Are you serious?" she croaks.

Serious about claiming that mouth, yeah.

I flash a wad of cash. "I'm gonna follow you around like your goddamn sugar daddy. Let's see how fast you can spend my money."

She starts walking, her silky hair swinging behind her. She tosses a look over her shoulder at me and I'm thrilled to see a playful light in her eyes. *Mission accomplished.* "Is there a bonus involved if I spend it before the fifty minutes are up?"

I shrug, noncommittal. "There might be other stipulations."

Merda. I didn't mean to start throwing sexual innuendos out, especially ones that make her sound like a whore, but she seems to like it, tossing her hair again with a smirk as she struts off.

She beelines it for a jewelry store and I smile. Clever girl. She knows she could spend the whole amount in one stop there. I'm all for it, if that's what she wants, but I also think she could use some practical shit, like a new pair of boots or a jacket. I glance around at the shops, to take in what they have. There's a boutique shoe store, and a couple clothing places.

I saunter after her into the jewelry store where she's already leaning over the glass cases. There's light in her face again, which eases the tension in my chest. She steals a glance over her shoulder at me, like she's making sure I'm not tricking her or making fun.

I lift my chin and raise my brows as if to say, "are you going to do it or not?"

She has a smile as she turns back to the case. She tries on a bunch of rings. I watch for a while to see what she likes, then walk around the store and look myself. There's a beautiful pink gem, emerald cut, set in 18K gold. It costs a little over two grand. I ask the woman behind the counter to bring it over to Desiree to see if she likes it.

She looks over at me in surprise when it arrives, then slips it on her finger and stares at it. "What is this gemstone?" she asks the attendant.

"Morganite. It's a cousin to emerald and aquamarine. It looks good on you."

"It does," I agree. I don't know why I picked it for her —it's not like she's a baby pink kind of woman. Maybe because it's both unique and stunning—like her.

Desiree looks from her finger to me, back to the attendant. "I'll take it." Her shoulders are thrown back, chin high.

I love her decisiveness. I pull out my wad of cash and count out 23 hundred dollar bills. "Does it fit? Do we need to get it sized for you?"

She twists it around her right ring finger. "It fits perfect."

I wink at her.

Cristo—have I ever winked in my life? I seriously doubt it. I'm not the winking type. That would be Stefano, my slick-talking youngest brother.

The clerk gives me my change, slips an empty ring box in a bag with the receipt, and hands it to us. "Enjoy."

"Seven hundred to go," I murmur to Desiree as we leave. "You like shoes?"

"I love shoes." There's color in her cheeks as we walk out—not a blush, just a flush of excitement. Desiree is definitely thriving on the retail therapy. Good. I may lack many qualities—manners, kindness, hands unsullied by blood, heart darkened by violence and pain, but I do have money. I'm not stupid enough to think I can buy her, but at least this one day I can give her something.

∼

Desiree

I should be ashamed of myself.

I *am* ashamed of myself. I shouldn't be getting turned on by a mobster buying me a giant rock for my finger.

It's my kid's birthday, he's spending it somewhere without me. Hopefully he's happy and safe and comfortable with his dad. Abe was never a bad dad. Never mean, or abusive or even too neglecting. I'm sure Jasper is safe and warm and fed. I imagine he's going to kindergarten somewhere—I sure hope he's in school, anyway.

But he sure as hell never bought me anything. He was a split it down the middle kind of guy right from the beginning. And once we got married, I always paid our bills, even when I was working my ass off to get through nursing school. He worked construction and spent his money on beer, and pot and eating out at greasy restaurants with his buddies.

Well.

Ashamed or not, it's a fact. My panties got damp when Junior pulled out that roll of money and spent over two grand on this ring. It feels heavy on my finger, catches the light when I swing my arms as I walk.

I'm feeling pretty damn loved right now. Oh God—not *loved*, loved. But yeah. Whatever. I may reject the word but the feeling's the same.

I head into the shoe store and browse around, totally conscious of Junior trailing behind me, watching my every move. They have a bunch of fancy shoes I would never wear. Well, I might wear them if I had a reason, but since my life consists of work, Zumba and home, I'm not interested in six-inch fashion heels.

Like in the jewelry store, Junior circles around the shop on his own trajectory and shows up at my side holding a nice leather boot. I already have a pair of boots —I'm wearing them—so I didn't even look at them. I drop my gaze to my own boots. Worn out. Fake leather. The style that came out three seasons ago.

"I'd like to try these in a seven," I tell the clerk.

She nods and heads off to the back room.

"So what? Now you're my personal shopper?" I should really act more grateful. Somehow, it's more fun pushing back at Junior, though.

As usual, he appears vaguely amused by my attitude, and just shrugs.

I try the boots on. They fit perfectly—totally comfortable. Three hundred fifty dollar price tag, not that it matters. Junior's buying.

"Well?" I demand.

"What so now you want my opinion?" The start of a smile tugs at one corner of his mouth.

"You are the personal shopper, aren't you?"

He full-on grins. "I'd take you shopping any day."

I don't know what to say to that. It's not like it's roses and chocolate sweet. But it kind of is.

I mean, don't guys hate shopping? Especially if it means the woman's spending all his money? And it's not like I'm being appreciative or nice or anything. It's not like he's getting anything out of this. Or does he think he is? I shoot him a suspicious look and his grin widens. Grows more feral.

Well shit. That should worry me, but instead it sets off butterflies of excitement in my belly.

"I'll take these," I tell the saleswoman. "Do you have them in brown as well?"

"I sure do!" she chirps and heads to the back room. She must work on commission.

"There," I tell Junior, who is looking through a rack of leather jackets. "All done, with time to spare."

Junior holds up a leather shearling jacket with black faux fur collar and cuffs. I never would've picked it out, but I try it on. It's comfortable and warm and ten times nicer than my current jacket. It costs $1029.

"I used up my budget already," I remind him.

"And this one, for when it's not as cold." Junior passes me a thinner, buttery leather slim cropped affair with a belt. It, too, is very comfortable and fashionable. And this puppy's four hundred bucks.

The saleswoman shows up, thrilled that I'm still shopping. "That looks so good on you," she gushes.

Junior waits until she toddles away, bringing my boots to the counter to murmur, "It does." He steps into my space and adjusts the collar, staring down at me with black eyes. "You like them? They're yours."

I lick my lips. "Why are you doing this?"

"To cheer you up. Is it working?"

I nod. "Yeah, actually. It is. Thanks."

He tilts his head down and for one second I think he's going to kiss me—and I'm not sure I'm into it, especially in a boutique, but he just leans his forehead against mine. "I don't like to see you cry," he murmurs.

My breath catches. I give his chest a very half-hearted push. More of a nudge really. "I didn't know you did nice."

He pulls away and I'm disappointed to see his mask's back in place, like I just reminded him to be an asshole. "You're right. I don't." No smile at all as he turns and walks to the counter, pulling out his money.

Damn. Why'd I have to be such a bitch?

∽

Junior

I SHOULD'VE GIVEN her a higher spending limit. I didn't realize she'd try to bust it all in one stop, but I don't mind seeing that ring flashing on her finger and knowing I put it there. Pretending I marked her with it, claimed her as mine.

She heads toward the car, but I make a negative sound in my throat. "Time's not up."

"Yeah, but I spent the limit."

I tip my head toward a clothing boutique. I'm an asshole, but I really want to see her changing clothes. Dressing up. Modeling shit. It's stupid, but a total turn on for me. I love the idea of a woman dressing for her man. Twirling around and asking if she looks good, knowing damn well she does.

She lifts her brows, but I can tell she likes it. A lot of women get turned on seeing money splashed around. I guess on a biological level, it shows the man's a good provider or some shit. All I know is throwing money down in front of a woman makes good foreplay. Not that I'm trying to get laid.

The boutique is all designer jeans—shelves and shelves of them with a few racks of designer tees in the middle of the store.

A young salesperson—the only one in the small shop—bustles over. "Can I help you find the perfect pair of jeans?"

Desiree throws a glance my way.

"Yes," I answer for her.

"Great, do you mind if I measure you?" The salesperson—who looks nineteen, and very serious about her jeans, whips out a measuring tape.

"Sure." Desiree pulls off her jacket and lifts her arms to get measured.

The salesperson fires off a series of questions about her preferences as she traipses about the shop, pulling a half dozen pairs of jeans from the shelves. "Let's start with these. Let me show you to the dressing room." She looks at me. "Do you want to go back with her?"

Fuck, yeah, I want to go back with her.

I give a solemn nod and palm a hundred dollar bill from my pocket. She leads us back and opens a curtain to a large changing room. Clearly we're the only ones in the shop, which suits me just fine.

As she leaves, I slip her the money and murmur, "Hundred bucks if you give us some time alone."

She tucks the money in her pocket. "You got it. Make a mess and you buy it." She arches a brow.

Cute. She has enough attitude to understudy Desiree.

I head into the dressing room where Desiree is already stripping off her boots, all business. She clearly didn't catch my exchange with the saleswoman.

I settle in one of the seats to watch the show.

"She didn't ask me if I wanted you to come back here," Desiree complains, stripping off her jeans.

"You did," I tell her. I know it's true by the confident way she undresses and struts over to pick up a pair of jeans to try on.

My mouth goes dry, dick gets hard as stone as I watch her try on a pair of jeans that hugs her ass.

"What do you think?" She turns around, looking critically in the mirror. Pretending she doesn't know she looks like a million bucks.

"We'll take them," I say, voice rough.

Her nipples get hard when she hears the desire in my voice and she shoots me a seductive look from under her lashes.

Beautiful woman.

She tries on another pair of jeans. They are equally magnificent. The third pair doesn't fit right. When she pulls them off, I get up from my seat, advancing with the stalking quality of a predator.

She goes still, watching me. Waiting for it.

I grasp her waist. "Get up there." I help her climb up to stand on the bench against the long wall of the dressing room.

"What are you doing?" She sounds breathless.

I push her ass back until it hits the wall, then pull the gusset of her panties aside, lower my head and taste her.

She jerks and cries out. I reach up and cover her mouth with one hand and yank her panties down and off with the other. She bucks her hips, gripping my arm for stability. Her open lips press against my palm, warm and soft.

I open her labia with my thumb and forefinger and trace around the inside, laving her clit, diddling it with the tip of my tongue, suctioning my lips over it and sucking.

She bites at my hand, moaning against it, her hot breath turning wet and steamy as she writhes under my tongue.

I don't stop torturing her. I lick and flick and work her swollen clit. I penetrate her with my stiffened tongue. She grips me by the hair and yanks me against her, pushing her sopping folds into my mouth. I shove two fingers inside her and she screams against my hand, which I clamp around her jaw even tighter. I'm being rough, but I know she likes it. Her body responds to me every fucking time, like it was made for me.

And right now, I'm going to make sure she comes faster than a freight train. Because she needs the release.

And damn, if I don't want to be the guy who gives it to her.

Every.

Fucking.

Time.

I curl my fingers inside her, trying to find her G-spot.

Bingo!

Her knees buckle and she cries out against my palm, pelvis jerking uncontrollably. I pump my fingers in and out. When I flick my tongue against her clit at the same time, she sobs and tears at my hair with one hand, her other hand grabbing my wrist to shove my fingers deeper. Her nails dig into my skin.

I pump a few times more to show her who's in control, then shove deep and give her a break long enough for her to come.

The moment I stop thrusting, she shudders and releases, her inner walls tightening around my fingers. She rises up on her tiptoes, squeezes her inner thighs together around my wrist. I keep lapping at her clit through her entire climax until she stumbles forward, and I have to catch her waist to keep her from falling. I slide my fingers out and help her down. I turn to sit on the bench and pull her onto my lap, palming her still pulsing pussy.

She moans and leans her head back on my shoulder. "Jesus, Junior."

I stroke her sopping folds like I'm soothing her pussy back to normal. "How do you feel now, doll?"

"Better," she murmurs. Her body is heavy on mine, like she's completely relaxed. "I hated being quiet, though."

Her laugh is husky, and it makes my aching dick throb even more. "I'm in the camp of if *I didn't scream, it didn't count.*"

I slap her pussy and her two thighs jerk together. "Didn't count?" I growl. I slap her wet folds again. "You need me to make it count?"

"Can we go back to your place?" Her voice rasps from the strangle-screaming. "Please?"

Fuck if I could deny her anything right now. Especially considering the state of my cock.

"So you can scream at the top of your lungs, baby?"

She gives another one of those husky laughs. "Yeah."

I lift her off my lap so fast she giggles and I slap her ass. "Ten seconds to get dressed," I bark.

She grabs her panties and hops around, putting them on.

I pick up the three pairs of jeans she hasn't tried on yet, plus the two that we know fit her. "I'm gonna pay for these. And I'm still counting." I put a little warning note in my voice for the last part and she grins, shoving her foot into her jeans.

"Right behind you, boss man."

Fuck, I am so lost for this girl.

∼

Desiree

Getting off without full-on penetration feels like cheating. I don't think I'd be happy as a lesbian because I really feel like I need the big cock. Of course, they make awesome dildos for that, so maybe I'd be fine.

All I know is I didn't get enough of Junior Tacone back in that clothing store, and I need to feel complete.

He drives back fast—screechy tires fast—and gets rid of Paolo. And then he grabs me outside Gio's room as soon as I finish repacking his wounds and refreshing the IV.

He shoves me up against the wall, pinning my wrists beside my head. His lips descend on mine, crushing my mouth. His teeth scrape my lips, tongue invades. All the while, he grinds his impressive erection against my belly.

I wrap one leg around his waist to angle him into the notch where he needs to be.

He curses in Italian and pulls my other leg up, then carries me into his bedroom.

I work open the button on the trousers of his thousand dollar suit and slide my hand down to grip his cock. It's long and hard and jerks in my palm. I drop to my knees while he frees his erection from his boxer briefs.

I'm wet just thinking about giving him pleasure. I part my lips and lift my gaze to his so I can watch his face the moment I take him into my mouth.

His eyes are dark as night and a muscle jerks in his face as I engulf the head, swirling my tongue underneath. He tunnels his fingers into my hair, grips it tight. I indulge in the fantasy of being forced.

I owe the mafia money and Junior's making me pay this way.

I take him deep into my throat, then pull back and rub my lips over the head a few times. I repeat it, gripping the base of his cock hard to make it lengthen down the back of my throat. I firmly cup and lift his balls, then stroke them downward a few times as I suck. Then I massage the taint, stroking from back to front.

Junior's breath turns ragged, his fist tightens in my hair. Pre-cum swirls in my mouth, mixing with my saliva to make a super-lube. I give his cock a moment to cool off and pump my hand over it as I suck his balls, lick along the line from the back of his testicles to his taint.

"You're fucking killing me," Junior rasps, his grip on my hair too tight. "I wanna come in your mouth so bad."

"So do," I tell him, positioning my lips over his cock again, but he holds my hair and pulls back.

"No, no, no, no. I need to fuck you, doll. I need to fuck you so hard you forget your name."

No arguments here.

He releases my hair and pulls me to stand by my elbow. "Bend over the bed." He slaps my ass as I turn to comply. He reaches under me to work the button on my jeans and I help him shove them down my hips. I hear the rip of a condom wrapper and then he shoves into me without preamble.

I cry out in pleasure.

This.

Yes.

Exactly what I need.

"Yes," I'm babbling right away. "Please, Junior, so good."

He grips my nape and plows in hard, slamming against my ass, his balls swinging against my clit.

I open my legs wider, arch my back to receive him. It

feels so good. Pleasure and satisfaction rocket through me, even though I haven't reached orgasm yet. My body sings, celebrating this new position, this moment. This man.

I cry out and moan and beg as he takes me fast and hard.

"You keep up that noise, I'm not gonna last much longer."

"Don't stop," I cry out. "I mean, come! Please, give it to me. Give it to me harder. Now."

I sound like the sluttiest porn character and I really don't care. All I know is I'm getting exactly what I need in this moment.

And it feels incredible.

"Fanculo, fanculo, fanculo, fuck!" Junior roars and slams deep into me. I swear I feel the heat of his cum, even through the condom.

I come too, ripples of pleasure rolling through my body as I milk his cock for all it's worth.

"Yes, Junior, yes." I'm still babbling.

Junior eases out and I float away, into the blessed space of no thought.

I return to reality when he cleans me with a washcloth and rubs my ass.

"You okay, baby?" The stern don is gone, replaced by the very human, very gentle side of Junior. It's a side I doubt he shows many, and I feel honored that he's shown it to me so many times today.

I roll to my side and sit up. My face feels hot. I push my hair out of my eyes. Junior hands me a bottle of water.

"You're the hottest fucking woman on the planet, you know that?"

I flush, drinking from the water bottle. "Thank you."

He smiles and puts a knuckle under my chin to lift my gaze. "You thanking me for the best sex I've had in years? Okay, I'll take it."

"Not for that. Well, yes for that, but just thank you." I find the courage to look him in the eye. "For today. For helping me forget."

"Forget what, baby?" he asks softly.

My eyes get wet, but it's okay. I don't feel sad anymore. Just wrung out. "Today's my little boy's birthday," I say, my throat squeezing. "And he's with his dad somewhere. And I don't know where." My voice wavers and breaks on the last word.

"Oh, baby." He pulls me up from the bed and into his arms, pulling up my panties and jeans while he holds me. It's a simple gesture, but I've never felt so taken care of in my life. At least not by a man. With Abe, I had to be his mama, not that he accepted anything I had to offer. But he certainly never gave. Never took care of me, even after I gave birth to his son. Never did me any favors.

I bury my face in Junior's chest and he rubs my back, cups the back of my neck, kisses my hair.

"I'm sorry, doll. I really am."

"So that's where my money goes. I've hired a private investigator to find them, but it's really expensive. And so far, my ex has kept under the radar."

"You're gonna find them." Junior's voice has a ring of conviction and I want so badly to believe him. "You will," he says firmly, like he knows I'm unsure. "And when you do, I'll be happy to take care of your ex for you."

My stomach knots and I push him away. "Junior, no."

He holds his palms up. "Well, if you ever need me to take care of him or *anyone*—you know I'd do it in a heartbeat."

I shake my head, fresh tears wetting my eyes, but this time they're not for me. At least I don't think they are. They're for him. For me because I can't have a man like him. It's not normal to suggest violence as a solution to every problem. And I don't think he even wants to be that man anymore. I don't think it's the real him. "Junior..."

"Yeah?"

"No." I try to keep the condemnation out of my voice, but don't quite succeed. When I see him flinch, I rush on. "I appreciate the offer, I really do. It's amazing to know I have someone like you in my corner." I reach out to touch his arm. "But I'm not down with the violence. And honestly? I don't think that's really you. I don't believe that's who you want to be. I mean, you told me you want out."

He scrubs a hand over his face, suddenly looking ten years older. "Yeah. Well. It's who I am, Desiree. I may hate it, but I can't change what is. And if I'm going to use violence for anything, it's sure as hell gonna be to help the woman I care about."

I don't think he meant to be so revealing, because he shoots a semi-alarmed glance at me, like he can't believe he said that.

The woman I care about.

The words hit me straight in the chest. The arrow

pierces, but it spreads warmth through my chest. It also scares the shit out of me.

We're not doing "care about" here. We were doing rough sex. I can't *care* about Junior Tacone. At least, I don't want to. There's no long term future for me with a mobster.

It must read it in my face, because he stands up, giving me his back.

The arrow lodged in my chest turns leaden.

But then a terrible thud sounds from Gio's room and Junior and I both go running out of the room.

CHAPTER 9

Junior

"Gio!" My brother's on the floor, groaning.

"Ow. Fuck." Gio groans.

I rush to his side and grab under his arm to help him up. "Hey, *fratellino*. Take it easy."

Desiree positions herself on the other side of him to help.

"I'm okay. 'S okay," Gio says, but he's panting and wincing and can't seem to stand up.

"*Fanculo*," I swear.

"On three," Desiree says, totally in charge of the situation, as usual. "One...two...three." I pull as hard as I can, because I sure as fuck know Desiree's not strong enough to lift my brother, and we get him up.

His yelp of pain goes right into the center my bones

though. My brother's no pansy. If he's making sounds like that, he's in serious pain, and can't control his own responses to it.

"On his left side," Desiree directs and we roll him over. She pulls off his bandage from the back, her lips forming a tight line.

"Is it okay?"

She uses her efficient nurse voice. "He tore the IV site and the stitches, but he'll be fine. I'll get him stitched and repacked."

Gio looks at his wound in the front. "How long since I was shot?"

"Four days," I tell him.

He cranes his head to look at Desiree. "I'm lying here with two holes in my gut while you're boning my nurse?" he asks me in Italian.

"Shut the fuck up," I say, but it doesn't have the force behind it I usually use. I'm relieved to hear Gio talk again.

"Well, she's hot, I'll give you that. I'd bang her—"

"I said shut up."

We're both speaking Italian, but Desiree gives us a suspicious look. "Are you talking about me?"

"He said you're beautiful."

Gio shoots me a startled look, like he can't believe I just made nice to another human being.

"That's the drugs talking," she says easily, and it occurs to me that it's not the first time a patient has said that to her. I have to swallow down a mouthful of jealous prickles. The kind that make me want to mark my territory so firmly no guy ever looks at her again.

I catch Gio studying me and attempt to make my face

blank. Or angry. Fuck—what did my face used to look like before Desiree? I don't feel like the same man I was a week ago.

"So who came over from Italy?" Desiree asks conversationally as her hands fly over the wound, cleaning, bandaging. "Your father?"

"Our grandfather moved the family over when our father was ten."

"And you all still speak fluent Italian?"

"He went back to Sicily to marry our mother—it was sort of an arranged thing, so we're first generation American on both sides," I explain and frown when I catch Gio watching me again.

"Where's Paolo?"

"He's around. Want to see him?"

"Nah, just making sure he's okay."

"Yeah, he's good. You were the only casualty on our side."

He glances at Desiree. "And on theirs?" he asks me in Italian.

"She speaks Spanish," I warn, also in Italian. Which means she can probably understand us. But I tell him, anyway. "All dead."

Desiree stiffens.

Fuck.

Gio nods and watches as Desiree preps his other arm for the IV. She inserts the needle and gets the drip running. Gio closes his eyes when the painkiller hits him, the taut lines of his face relaxing.

"You want the TV on or anything?" I ask, but he doesn't even open his eyes, just shakes his head, sinking into rest again.

I look at Desiree. Things are getting too intense between us. Every minute I'm with her I fall in deeper—and I can't. As much as I want to claim Desiree forever, she wants—needs—a different man. And if I'm going to let that happen—let her walk away when this is all through, I need to stop acting like we're dating or a couple. We need a chance to catch our breaths. No wine and pasta and a hard fucking on the countertop tonight. But the what-to-do options are pretty limited considering how housebound we both are. "How about pizza and a game of gin rummy?" I suggest as we walk out of Gio's room.

She shoots me a funny look. "Um, yeah. Okay." Her voice sounds surprised, but willing.

"Joker's wild," I tell her.

Her soft laugh is sweet and yielding. "Joker's wild."

CHAPTER 10

Desiree

I WAKE up on the wrong side of the bed the next morning. I don't know—maybe it's just too much for me to process—grieving my little boy, being held in quasi-imprisonment by Junior. Having feelings for said captor and not wanting them.

I'm mixed up, muddled up, miffed.

I do my usual rounds with Gio, then shower and dress. Instead of looking for breakfast, I put on my new leather jacket and walk out the front door. I need a break from the house and I'm feeling prickly about still being a prisoner, even though Junior treated me like a princess yesterday.

I'm not surprised to hear the door fly open behind me. *"Hey."* It's a sharp, commanding bark.

I'm not dumb enough to keep walking. I stop, but don't turn around.

"Where are you going?" Junior strides purposefully toward me. He's already showered and dressed himself, looking impeccable as always in a finely tailored suit.

"Back off, bossman." I give it right back to him. "I'm going for a walk."

It's not cute foreplay this time. I'm not feeling sassy, I'm downright bitchy, and he's not amused. "Don't speak to me that way." It's a low command. The kind that is certain of being obeyed.

I find myself flushing, because he really doesn't deserve my nastiness. Not today, anyway. Still, I don't back down. "Listen," I tell him, hands on my hips. "I'm doing my job. I'm all in on taking care of Gio. I'm trusting you to hold up your end of the bargain and pay me and let me go when he's up and around. But trust goes both ways. You show a little, too. I need some fresh air, so I'm taking it. I'll be back in twenty minutes, okay?"

His mouth firms into a thin line and he stares at me for a long moment. He looks as weary today as I feel. After a moment, he tips his head in the direction I was walking, as if to say, "then go."

I turn and flounce off, walking with long, angry strides —the kind designed to burn off frustration. I don't look back until I'm halfway down the block, and when I do, I find Junior trailing twenty feet behind me.

Nope. No trust on his part.

He's probably freezing his ass off without a coat, too.

I'm not going to feel bad about it. He's the one who

decided I needed to be supervised on my walk around the block.

Or three. I walk a long loop and by the time I arrive back at the house, I'm feeling more like myself. More awake. Alive. A little sassy. A little sorry.

I stop at the sidewalk leading up to his million dollar house and look back at my tail. It's ridiculous what the sight of him does to me. The flutters in my chest at his large, fit frame, flutters in my belly over his frown.

Because I still think I'm right and don't want to say sorry, but I also want to make nice, I wait for him. When he arrives, my body moves toward him of its own accord, and suddenly I'm leaning my forehead against his chest. It's not quite surrender—more like beating my head against a wall.

And that wall is him.

It takes two beats before his arms lift and circle me. "You okay?" His gruff voice holds genuine concern.

I nod against his chest. "A little out of sorts."

He rubs the back of my neck. "Me too." He pulls me away from his chest and grips my jaw, tilting my face up. And then his lips descend on mine, his kiss a punishment —hard and claiming.

I yield to it, open my lips to let his tongue sweep in.

He starts off hard, but by the time he's finished, his lips and tongue are in exploration, tasting me, teasing me. When he breaks it, I've forgotten why I was in a snit. He stares down at me. His expression is inscrutable, but his thumb strokes my cheek lightly.

"What's your real name?" I ask, somewhat breathlessly.

It's like I need something from him—some concession, something personal.

Something stiffens in his face. "Santo." He doesn't like saying the name. Maybe it reminds him of his father, and the memories aren't good.

I know he feels trapped by his father—I felt it in every word he spoke about his situation. That's why I encouraged him to leave it all.

It had nothing to do with me trying to make him into someone I could be with long term.

Nothing at all.

I shiver and he turns me toward the house. "Let's get some breakfast." We head into the house and then straight through to the garage.

"My car!"

It's there beside his beautiful Maserati. I had worried about it sitting in the hospital parking lot, but never imagined it was right here the whole time. That kind of makes escape plans more simple—not that I'm still plotting that sort of thing.

"Yeah. I wanted it somewhere safe," Junior says. "Don't get any ideas," he warns, ruining any appreciation I might have felt for his thoughtfulness.

He opens the door to the Maserati and reaches across me to put the keys in the ignition. "Start it up if you get cold. I'll be right back."

Well. That's a sliver of trust, isn't it? He left me with the keys in the ignition. I could totally take the car and leave.

Of course, he'd kill me.

Literally.

So he probably knows I'm not going any further than a walk around the block without his permission. And that's why I really need to stop turning molten every time he touches me.

∾

Junior

I GRAB twenty grand in cash and jump in the car with Desiree, who has her pop music playing on the radio.

I don't know why I find that so adorable.

Her barb this morning about not trusting her stuck in my ribs. She's right. I don't. I can't. That's how I was raised. The training drilled into me by Santo Tacone.

But I brought her an olive branch. I drop her phone in her lap.

She looks over at me in surprise, but I don't acknowledge it. Fuck, my suspicious instincts already have me wanting to snatch it back, keep her from any outside contact.

But I have to trust her at some point. If I'm letting her walk out of my house when it's all through, trusting her not to tell anyone, then I should extend the same faith now.

Still, when she immediately starts texting someone, I get tense. She's a fucking saint, because she says to me in an exasperated voice, "I'm texting Lucy, my bestie from work. Just to tell her I miss her ass." She holds up the screen to prove it.

"Thanks," I mutter.

I drive all the way into the city, to Caffè Milano. Kill two birds with one stone.

I circle the block, looking for anything off. Cops could be watching the place after the shooting. Or Vlad's crew. Once again, I probably should've called one of the guys to watch my back. I would've insisted Gio or Paolo bring backup if they'd come. It goes against my alpha tendencies to admit any weakness, though. I don't see anything or anyone who looks out of place, so I pull in and shut off the ignition.

"You're actually going to leave your Maserati parked on a street in this neighborhood?" Desiree asks in disbelief.

I shrug. "Used to be everyone in this neighborhood knew better than to mess with my car. Not sure if that's still the case, but I'm gonna hope so."

"May I drive it?" she asks as she slams the door shut.

"What?" I'm taken aback, mostly because no one in their right mind has ever asked me to drive it, other than my *stronzo* brothers, and I told them all to fuck themselves twenty times before finally relenting.

She beams a thousand-watt smile at me as I head to her side, protectively shielding her from traffic. "Pretty please, Junior? Come on, what does it do—zero to one hundred in four seconds?"

I chuckle, surprised at her interest and knowledge. "Yeah."

"Let me drive it. Please? I'll give you the best cock-suck in the history of the universe."

My dick goes rock hard at her proposal. I have to

JOKER'S WILD

reach down and adjust myself in my pants. "Well, fuck. That's a tough offer to refuse." I grip her face and kiss her again, like I did in front of my house this morning. I don't know what my fascination is with kissing her so much, but I can't seem to stop. She tastes like mint toothpaste and berry lip balm. Her lips are soft and full, and so fucking luscious. Seriously, I want to eat her up.

And yeah, I am the big, bad wolf.

I shouldn't. We're not a couple. This isn't dating. We have an arrangement, but I know she's not interested in continuing beyond its expiration.

"Is that a yes?" she asks when I break the kiss. I love her spunk.

"Yes." I can't look away. She's all bright-eyed and flushed—so full of life. Such contrast to me. I've been half-dead for years. For sure since Mia's death, but probably longer. Hell, I can't remember when my life ever felt worth living. Like it was my own.

I'll bet Nico doesn't feel that way. That *testa di cazzo* has been living his own life since the day he graduated high school and cooked up his Vegas plan.

I force myself to break the eye contact, to sweep the streets for anything dangerous. Any observers. I don't see anything off. Even so, I get the sweats when we walk up to Caffè Milano, the echo of shots ringing in my ears. The sound Gio made when hit. The look on his face flashes before my eyes. And then the image of the carnage I left behind.

I'm not innocent. I've had blood on my hands before. But that scene was pretty fucking bad. I didn't even know I had it in me to be a one-man Terminator. I guess that's what happens when someone shoots my brother.

The place has a few customers ordering their morning coffee at the bar. Some young people sit at tables with their computers out. An old man reads a newspaper.

"So are you going to tell me what's going on?" Desiree asks in a low voice.

"What do you mean?" I ask without stopping my constant sweep of the area. I draw in a slow breath, but my heart's still beating too hard.

"Are we here for business? Because you sure don't look hungry."

Cazzo. I shouldn't have brought her. What in the hell was I thinking? She's already an accessory. Now I'm just further burying her.

"Baby, don't ask questions."

"Are you freaking kidding me?" She keeps her voice low, but the tone is every level of pissed off. "Junior, I don't want to be a part of this shit."

I scrub a hand over my face. "I know. I fucked up. I shouldn't have brought you. I don't know what I was thinking."

Actually, I do know what I was thinking. That having her along would ease the strain. Maybe even help me smooth things over with the Milano family, because she's the type who can lead anyone she wants around by the nose.

Myself included.

The Milano girl is behind the counter, and goes pale when she sees me, but otherwise plays it cool.

Desiree and I go to the counter and order coffee and

pastries, then sit down at one of the tables. Now that I'm inside, I check out the new glass. It's decent. Thick, double-pane. Better than what they had in here before.

That's good.

I pick up a newspaper from one of the tables and pretend to read the headlines. I'm thinking I'll slip the money into the newspaper and hand it to the granddaughter before we leave.

"Junior, I'm scared."

I look up, surprised. Desiree doesn't strike me as the type to admit her feelings, especially one like fear.

"What are we doing here? What's going to happen?"

I reach across the table and pick up her hand. It's ice cold. "Baby, you don't have to be scared." I don't know what compels me—I've never spilled a secret in my life—but I can't stand the thought of her nervous because of me.

She probably picked up on my PTSD being here and now she thinks something terrible is going down.

"This is the place Gio got shot," I tell her in a low voice. "I came to make nice with the owners, that's all."

Now Desiree's face is pale. She darts her eyes around without moving her head, like she's a spy or something. "Okay," she nods a few times, as if she's trying to be brave. "What do we have to do?"

Her words hit me square in the chest. Shock me.

What do we have to do.

Even though I subconsciously brought her to be my better half, to be a part of my team, it was the wrong thing to do. And yet here she is, terrified, out of her element, disapproving of the whole thing, but still willing to play my sidekick.

I squeeze her cold fingers. "You don't have to do anything. I just wanted to show my face and leave some cash to cover damages. I'm gonna put it in this newspaper and hand it to our waitress when she comes."

Again, the over-share shocks me.

My own father would shoot me in the head for being so fucking stupid.

Maybe this is what love does to you.

Fuck.

Do I love Desiree?

I sure as hell don't remember feeling this way about Marne. I cared for her—still do—but it's in more of an abstract way. The way I feel for Desiree is visceral. Real. Like I'd rather stab myself in the eye than see her hurting. Or scared. And she demanded my trust, so I'm giving it to her.

I'm also placing her in all kinds of danger.

Which is why this isn't going to work. I need to stay the fuck away from Desiree or I'll drag her right down to the depths of hell with me.

"You should quit this business, Junior. You don't like it," she says, like she read my mind.

The truth of her words hit me hard.

I've spent most of my life feeling sick over who I am. What I do. I'm a monster. I gunned down six Russians in this cafe, for Christ's sake. Yes, they meant to kill us first, but is this any way to live?

And maybe when I said my dad wouldn't have an identity without it, I was really talking about myself.

Sure, I'd love to just shut down shop. Move my mom to Florida and spend the rest of my days watching girls in bikinis. But the emptiness in that idea leaves me cold. What in the hell would I do with myself? What would I live for?

If my daughter Mia was still alive, maybe I'd feel different.

Maybe I'd still have a decent marriage, having something besides a dying business to look after.

"You could go legit like Nico did. Open a string of Italian restaurants in the old neighborhoods so you can look after things."

"No?" She watches me closely, like she's trying to tune into my thoughts. I'm not used to people trying to read me. To anyone giving a shit what I think unless it affects them.

I adjust our table to fix the wobble in it. "I don't know, doll. The pressure I feel from my dad is fucking real. But yeah, I'd like to get out of *La Nostra*. I really would."

"Then you should."

I stare at her, feeling like I'm thrust backward, away from her and any possibility of a normal, legit life. A normal family. A woman who makes the room light up. It's like I'm in a movie, when the camera suddenly zooms way, way back. She becomes tiny. So far away. Completely out of reach.

And I'm here, stuck being the man everyone hates. My own brothers included.

The Milano girl comes over. "Here you go, Mr. Tacone," she murmurs as she places my coffee in front of me.

"You okay?" I ask.

She heaves in a breath and blows it out. "Yeah." A bob of her head. "I'm okay."

"Baby, this is Ms. Milano, owner of the place." I purposely don't use Desiree's name. And of course, I'm not sure of the Milano girl's first name. Under the table I slide the envelope of cash into the newspaper.

"Marissa."

Ah. That had been one of my guesses.

She slides our pastry plates down. "My gramps still owns it. I just run it for him."

"How is Luigi?"

"Good, good. Well. He's getting old. He's a little pissed off at you right now, too. Says you're letting the neighborhood go to hell." She glances nervously around and gives a forced little laugh.

The familiar thud of guilt hits me like a wrecking ball, square in the chest. "Yeah, I'm working on it," I tell her.

"Junior won't be around forever," Desiree cuts in, eyes sparking. "There's a season for everything, you know? And his season might be winding down."

I stare at Desiree, shocked by her instinct to defend me.

Marissa flushes.

I thrust the folded newspaper at her. "Here, you can take this," I hold her eye so she knows I'm communicating something more than a garbage run. "I'm all done with it."

She nods and spins around to walk away, moving swiftly toward the back room.

I drain my coffee. "doll, I'm not used to anyone being crazy enough to speak for me." My voice comes out gruff, but it's not a remonstration. I'm just not used to feeling indebted to people.

"Well, that's bullshit," she snaps and I can't help but smile.

"You're still dreaming I can quit."

"You want to. Admit it."

I find myself drawing in a sudden breath at the audacity of even allowing myself to *think*, much less *speak* that truth.

I ball up my napkin and toss it on the table. "I can't. End of story." I stand up.

Marissa emerges from the back room and gives me a nod from behind the counter. I guess that means I brought enough. I walk over and hand her a card. "Tell Luigi to call me if he needs anything, yeah?"

She takes the card and bobs her head.

"Or you can call. Caffè Milano is a business I will always support."

I mean *protect*, but I don't want to say it out loud in front of customers.

"I appreciate that, Mr. Tacone, I really do."

Desiree steps closer to me and I put a hand on her back.

"Have a nice day," I say, steering Desiree toward the door.

"You too. Thank you," the Milano girl sings out to my back as we leave.

"So what's her story?" Desiree asks rather sharply as we walk out.

I shrug. "Don't know. I remember her running around here as a little kid. Now she's running the place."

"The money made her moony." There's a bitterness in Desiree's voice that isn't familiar to me.

I stop her in front of my car and tilt my head, looking down into her face. "What do you mean?"

She purses her lips. "Like she was ready to blow you after she saw how much you gave her."

A bark of surprised laughter tumbles out of me. "*Cavalo*, doll. You don't have to be jealous. I'll be giving you twice that." I smile. "And you won't even have to blow me." Except all the blood rushes to my dick at learning Desiree's jealous, so I'm immediately sorry for those words.

She flushes and gives me a shove, like she's embarrassed at being called out. "I'm not jealous," she grumbles.

I back her against my car, cage her between my arms. "Baby, I'd give you money just for that pretty smile of yours." I grind against her, watching her pupils dilate, the pulse in her neck go wild and frantic.

She grips the lapels of my jacket in her small fists and pulls me even tighter against her, rocking her hips to meet mine. "Yeah?"

"Yeah. I even said I'd let you drive my car, and you should know that I don't let *anybody* drive my car."

She beams up at me. "Then give me the keys, hot shot."

I shove my aching cock into the notch between her legs one more time, then dig my hand into my pocket to produce the keys. "Please don't make me sorry," I beg. "This car is my baby."

Her grin is naughty as hell, and she's every bit the woman who drives me wild—the sassy, confident beauty who tosses her hair and swings her hips as she walks, daring every man around to watch her without getting hard.

I groan and pull open the passenger door, sliding in.

~

Desiree

Junior's on edge as I pull out onto the street. One hand clutches the car door handle, one is balled in a fist on his lap. I gun it, to test how fast it takes off and we sail into traffic.

I drive like I'm in a car race—because when else will I get to drive a car like this?

It takes a few minutes, but Junior starts to relax. His fist unclenches and he stops watching the road like something terrible is about to happen.

"Nice driving, doll." He sounds surprised. Impressed, even.

I grin at him. "What? You didn't think a woman could handle a car like this?"

His lips quirk. "You don't get to drive my car *and* bust my balls, sugar."

I love when he gets bossy with me. It does something hot and tingly to my whole body.

"I told you I don't let anyone drive this car. Ever. Consider yourself privileged."

That news shouldn't make me so happy. It's not like he just swore his undying love to me, but it's nice to know

I'm special. I like thinking he makes special concessions just for me.

I take a turn way too fast, letting the tires squeal. My nipples are hard, the speed and danger turning me on.

"I'm going to give you the best blowjob, Junior," I promise.

He groans and leans back in his seat, rearranging his junk.

"Where do you want it?"

"Excuse me?"

"Where do you want the blowjob? In this car? Or is too precious for you to have sex in."

Junior growls, squeezing his dick through his pants with what looks like brutal force. "Oh, you're going to blow me in this car. But I'm gonna be in that driver's seat."

I laugh. "Of course you are."

"What'd I say about busting my balls?"

"I don't know, I kinda consider it my job. I'm not sure you get nearly enough ballbusting in your life."

Junior's heavy-lidded gaze rests on my face and I swear I detect nothing but fondness in it. Fondness and heat.

Which works for me, because driving Junior's car is total foreplay for me. I'm so turned on by the time I pull into his garage, I'm ready to strip my clothes off and throw myself at him. But I promised a blowjob, and I intend to make it good.

I turn off the motor and climb over the center console, onto Junior's lap.

His hands grip my hips. "What are you doing, doll?"

I put my tits in his face. "Changing places," I say with

mock innocence. "Didn't you want to be in the driver's seat?"

His cock lengthens under my lap.

"Not sure I can walk at the moment," he admits, lifting my hips and grinding me down over his erection.

My panties are wet, nipples harder than diamonds. I grab the door handle and open the door. I climb out and lean over him, hands on his thighs. "Maybe you'd better stay where you are, then."

Junior tilts the seat back and shifts his knees toward me. "Maybe I'd better." His voice is gravelly and low.

I unbutton his pants and free his erection. Junior fists the base of it, holding his full length out to me.

I reach for the tin of mints in his center console and pop one in my mouth. "Tell me if you like the tingle." I open my lips to take him in.

His cock jerks and grows even fatter as I slide my lips over it. "Oh fuck." Junior lifts his hips to shove deeper into my throat. "I really fucking like the tingle."

I hum softly as I move my mouth up and down his length, relaxing my throat and taking him deeper each time.

"Oh my God. You're killing me," he growls when I get faster.

I pop off and pay some attention to his balls, licking and sucking them while I let his cock cool in the air. When I put my mouth back over it and take him deep, he shouts.

"That's right. *Cristo*. You keep working that hot little mouth, doll. Gonna make me come so hard."

I suck as hard as I can, ignoring the ache in my jaw as I

give it all I have. I want to make this good for Junior. It turns me on to witness the effect I have on him. I cup his balls, massage behind them over his prostate as I bob my head faster and faster.

"Don't stop. Oh God, don't stop," he groans. His cock lurches, balls draw up. "I'm gonna come."

Hot streams of his salty essence hit the back of my throat and I swallow it down, like I promised. I lick him clean and then smile wide, pleased with myself.

"Desiree, doll, you can drive my car anytime," he says and we both laugh.

CHAPTER 11

*D*esiree

On the sixth day of Gio's recovery, he spikes a fever. I check his temperature with the thermometer from my med kit, then his blood pressure.

Temperature of one hundred three and elevated blood pressure.

Crap.

I don't know if it was the fall out of bed, or ripping the stitches, or what, but I don't like it. In fact, it worries the hell out of me.

I'm not a doctor. I have no idea what that bullet hit inside Gio. And if something's infected, all the progress he made this week will be lost. He could easily still die.

"Junior," I call from Gio's room.

He must hear the fear in my voice because he shows up immediately. "What is it?"

"Gio spiked a fever. I'm going to need a new antibiotic—see if you can get Keflex. Or clindamycin, but that's going to give him the shits. And salty soup."

He studies my face, and must read how serious this is because he's all business. "I'll go now. Anything else?"

I shake my head, going to the bathroom to get warm wash cloths to try to cool Gio down.

Junior leaves. It occurs to me that it's the first time he's left me alone, but that's so irrelevant right now. Either he trusts me, or he figures this is an emergency and he has no other choice. It doesn't matter—I have bigger things to worry about.

I give Gio a sponge bath with warm water, then sit beside him. I've lost patients before. There are times it breaks my heart, no matter how hard you try to remove yourself from it.

But losing Gio is not an option.

There's no way I could watch that happen. No way I could witness Junior's pain.

I get Gio to swallow a little Tylenol and run the possibilities in my head. The fact that his body was healing and took a turn for the worse concerns me. It will be at least twenty-four hours before I know if a new antibiotic works. In that time, he could go septic.

Shit.

Maybe I should talk Junior into taking him to a hospital. Although they would probably do the same thing I'm doing here.

I pick up my phone. There's one person I ask for help in cases where it seems like patients need something beyond medicine.

My mom.

And she doesn't go into work until this afternoon.

I call her up and speak to her in Spanish. "Mamá, I need some help. My patient had a fall yesterday that reversed his recovery. Do you think you could come and do some of your Reiki magic on him?"

"Of course, *mija*." That's the amazing thing about my mom. If someone calls for her services, she never refuses. She believes it's a gift from God that she's obligated to share wherever it's needed.

"I'm at a house in Oak Park. Can you come this morning before your shift?"

"Yes," my mother says slowly. "Yes, I can come. What's the address?"

"I'll text it to you. Can you come right now?"

"Yes, I'll come right now," my mom says, surprised, like she doesn't know why I'm asking again.

"Okay, I love you, Mom. See you in a bit."

"*Hasta luego,* bye." My mom says in her customary Spanglish.

Relief pours through me. I've seen my mom perform miracles before. Quiet ones. The kind that people don't even notice because it's not in their frame of reference to attribute a sudden turnaround to a hands-on energy healing. And my mom doesn't care if they acknowledge it or not. She doesn't get attached to results. She just gives and says she gets something out of the act of giving. She receives at the same time, and that's enough.

I pace around the house, my stomach in knots. Junior left one of his goons here—one of the guys who grabbed me from the parking lot, but I think I can handle him.

Junior said he was here for protection, not to keep me prisoner. I'm just hoping my mom gets in and out before Junior shows up, because I know he's going to freak.

I consider texting him, but I sort of chicken out.

This situation is serious, and I had to make a tough decision. My mom won't pay attention to how Gio got his wound or why I'm treating him at home. She may put it together, but it won't even matter to her.

She's just not like that. She sort of operates in a bubble of kindness, my mother.

She shows up forty minutes later and I rush down the stairs to let her in.

"It's okay, it's my mom. She's here to help," I tell the bodyguard, who has drawn a pistol.

He gives me a doubtful look. "Junior know about this?"

"Of course he does," I snap, using my customary bluster to get the guy to back off. Fortunately, he does. He opens the door a crack and when he sees it's my mom, puts the gun away.

She envelops me in a warm hug, kissing both my cheeks.

"Here he is." I lead her upstairs, wringing my hands. "He'll go on a new antibiotic today, but I don't like the way he's burning up."

My mom pulls up a chair beside the bed and puts one hand on Gio's shoulder, the other on his hand. "Ay, he is hot, isn't he? We'll see what we can do." She closes her eyes. I watch for a moment.

I swear I feel my own worries drain away as my mom works. Like the energy is healing me at the same time.

When I was in high school and I'd come home all upset

about something, she'd tell me to sit down, and she'd put her hands on my shoulders and within fifteen minutes, all my angst would drain away.

I'm sure some day they'll discover the science around energy healing—I even read a great book about a guy who could consistently and repeatedly cure mice of cancer—but I'm still content to believe she's magic.

After twenty minutes, I'm completely soothed. The energy in the room pulses with a fine, pure vibration. My mom shifts her hand to lightly cover Gio's wound, even though the blanket's up, and I didn't tell her where it was. She just sees where to go.

She lifts her hand above the area, flicking her fingers like she's brushing away the heat. She circles her hand over it. Lifts and lowers it. It goes on for a while, but I don't leave. The energy feels too pleasurable not to stay and witness the healing.

After another ten minutes, she stands up and waves her hands over his entire body, like she's building an energy cocoon around him. Finally, she backs up, toward me and the door.

She turns to me and nods with a serene smile.

I hug her. "*Gracias, Mamá*. I love you so much."

"And you?" she asks, pulling away and peering up at my face. "All good?"

I nod, hoping I won't flush. I'm sure I've changed in the days since I've been here. I've had more sex than I've had in years. My emotions have been tested in all directions. I may be falling in love against my own will.

My mom nods as if satisfied by what she sees in my face. "Okay, I'm going. Have to get some lunch before my shift. I love you." She gives me another two kisses on my cheeks.

I lead her downstairs and open the front door, congratulating myself for getting her in and out of here before Junior gets back.

And that's when I see Junior's car pull into the drive.

∽

Junior

It takes me four stops to find a connection to give me the prescription Desiree asked for. I have to say, I'm scared as hell, because Desiree seemed to be on high alert, the way she was when she first got to my house and helped get Gio stabilized.

I admire the fuck out of how clear and professional she is, even when worried. I guess that comes with her job.

There's a strange car parked in front of my house, which puts me on even higher alert. I sent Luca over to guard Gio and Desiree while I was gone, because we still haven't found Vlad, but that's not his car. His is in front of it. I park in the drive and draw my Beretta as I get out of the car.

The front door moves, like it had just been open a crack and someone shut it.

Holy fuck.

All I can think is that Vlad showed up for his revenge. Who else could it be? I run for the front door, gun

JOKER'S WILD

palmed along my leg. I grip the handle and turn it slowly.

It swings open abruptly. "Hi, Junior," Desiree chirps in a falsely cheerful voice.

I'd lifted the gun, but I lower it, because she's the only body in front of me. I step into the house, peering past her at…

An older woman.

A short Hispanic woman with salt and pepper hair and Desiree's eyes.

I put the safety on my gun and shove it in my pocket.

"I called my mom," Desiree says breathlessly and the room suddenly spins around me.

What the fuck?

Black bleeds around my vision.

Was this some elaborate escape plan of hers? Did she make up Gio's condition? I *trusted* her.

I give my head a shake, drawing in a harsh breath.

No, he really had a fever. I felt him myself.

"My mom does energy work, and I wanted her to work on Gio. Sometimes her treatments make all the difference in a person's healing."

Wait...what? I narrow my eyes, trying to understand what the fuck Desiree is talking about. She's speaking in rushed sentences that are too hard for me to follow. Or maybe it's my brain is too slow right now.

"Mamá, this is my employer, Mr. um, Jones. Mr. Jones, my mother, Flor de Liz Lopez."

Mr. Jones. Okay, she's trying to cover for me. But the woman is at my house. And just saw my wounded brother. She's a witness.

Luca appears from the living room, totally relaxed. Dumb fuck. "You need me to stick around, boss?"

I just shake my head, because if I speak, I'm going to be a serious asshole.

Luca steps through the door and Desiree catches it and holds it open. "My mom's gotta run to her shift at the hospital. Bye, Mom!" She shuffles her mom past me and practically shoves her out, shutting the door tight behind her.

Two seconds go by as I try to decide if I need to go after her or not.

But Desiree's standing in front of me, twisting her hands. "Just chill out, Junior," she says, but her words are pleading. "She doesn't know anything. She didn't see the wound, didn't ask any questions. She just shows up and does her thing and leaves. Nothing to worry about."

I take a step toward Desiree. I suppose it must come off as menacing, because she takes two steps back, her pupils narrow with alarm. I can't reassure her, because I'm still teetering on the edge of doubt.

And the idea of Desiree not being trustworthy fucking guts me.

I don't even know what I'd do.

I couldn't hurt her. I don't even think I have it in me to threaten her with something awful.

"What were you thinking?" I snarl. "You just made your mom a witness."

"Junior, you're not listening. *She saw nothing.* And even if she knew everything, you're safe. *She's my mom.* Her trust lies with mine. Always. I'm on your side, I'm Team Tacone, so that means she is, too. Without question, without a shadow of a doubt. We're family." She tilts her head. "Surely you understand about that?"

The haze around my vision starts to clear and I draw in a few deeper breaths.

I'm Team Tacone.

I'm on your side.

Her words do something terrible and beautiful to me. Shred me in half and reshape me into something new.

And suddenly I'm on her, kissing the fuck out of her, holding the back of her head captive as my tongue sweeps into her mouth. I nip her lips, suck them. Bruise them with the intensity of my desire.

I carry her upstairs, legs wrapped around my waist, never breaking the frantic kiss. In my bedroom, I lower her to stand and rip her scrubs off while she works on my clothes. I bite her neck, lift her up and throw her on her back on my bed.

I want to reward her for hours, but there's too much pressure built up—like my whole life, my whole essence of being just undammed and wants to pour out to her. There's no stopping it. I yank off her panties and shove one knee up to feast between her legs. It's not nuanced foreplay—I'm not capable of precision. It's more like I devour her. Suck and bite and plunge my tongue in her entrance. And then I can't wait any longer. I yank off my boxer briefs and roll on a condom in record time and then I'm over her.

Spearing her with my erection.

Claiming her with every ounce of my being.

I slam in hard. She cries out, but her eyes are closed, her head tipped back with pleasure.

Fuck, I need her. I plant my hands up above her shoulders so she can't slide and fuck her with all the force inside me. It's rough.

Rabid.

It's far more animal than man.

I didn't know I had this amount of passion in me, but here it is. Pouring out, mingling with hers, making me a new man. Whole again.

She's making her noises—cries and moans and incoherent begging.

"Desiree," I choke. Because I need to speak her name. The name of the woman who did this to me. Who turned me inside out. Reshaped me.

Her eyes open and she reaches for me. Digs her nails into my back as I slam into her supple body. She wraps her legs around my waist and hooks her ankles behind my back, using her legs to encourage me even deeper, harder. To show me she wants this. Wants more.

And I don't hold back. The bed slams against the wall, mattress bounces and shakes as I take my woman, give her every ounce of everything I have.

A stream of Italian comes out of my mouth. I'm babbling more than she is. My thighs tighten up, lightning strikes at the base of my spine. I roar like a fucking lion, slam in and out of her so hard I fear I'll break her. And then I go deep.

"Fuck, Desiree, come, baby." I'm begging her to come because I can't hold my orgasm back, and I don't have the coordination or brain cells to make sure she gets off.

She does. Her muscles tighten and squeeze my dick the minute I tell her to, a quick pulsing that makes her choke on a scream, head thrown back, eyes rolled up in her head.

I fill the condom. Fuck, I come so much I fear it won't hold it all. And then I'm on top of her, panting into her neck, listening to her slowing cries.

"Did you get the antibiotic?" she asks after a moment and I curse and pull out. "Yes. Yeah, I got it." I dispose of the condom and fish the antibiotic out of my coat pocket.

Desiree pulls on her scrub bottoms without panties and my undershirt.

I smile, satisfaction at seeing her in my clothes surging. I hand her the antibiotic and yank on my own clothes, then follow her into Gio's room.

She's already injected it into the IV. "Look," she says softly, lifting her chin toward Gio. "He already looks better. I'm not that religious, but I swear my mom has a direct line to God. Or source energy—whatever you want to call it."

I go still. I hadn't even understood what she'd told me before. About why she called her mom here. But she's right. There's none of the usual pained restlessness around Gio. The lines of his face have softened, and he looks peaceful. His breath is steady. I touch his head. Still warm, but not burning as hot as this morning.

I pull Desiree into me and kiss the top of her head. And then, because she's braless and her nipples are popping through my thin shirt, I have to palm her breast. Have to rub my thumb over the pebbled tip.

And then I'm squeezing her ass.

"Is my punishment over?" she asks, her lips curving into that taunting smile I love so much.

I work my finger between her ass cheeks, which is easy since she's only wearing scrubs— no panties. "Baby, that wasn't punishment," I murmur. "That was your reward. Punishment comes later." I curl my finger to touch her anus, showing her exactly how I'll be taking her to task.

She moves restlessly, and I cup my other hand around her mons to stimulate her both places. Her breath comes in short pants. I release her, it was just a tease to keep her on edge. I'm still soaring from her revelation. Still soaked in gratitude, wanting to reward her in every way possible.

∾

Desiree

Um, wow.

I seriously don't even know what just happened.

One minute I'm freaking out, trying to make Junior understand my mom's not a threat, the next minute he's pounding into me like the world's going to end, and it's our last chance at having sex. Ever.

The whole time I couldn't figure out if it was punishment or reward.

No, I guess I knew it wasn't punishment. It may have been the roughest sex I've ever had, but what came out of him was pure passion. I just have no idea what triggered it.

I go back to his bedroom and get myself properly

dressed. He's in the walk-in closet, standing in front of what must be an open safe.

When he comes out, he tosses three big stacks of cash on the bed. "That's for you."

"Wait...what is this?" I don't know why, but the money comes as a shock—and not a pleasant one. "Are you getting rid of me?" What the hell is going on? Was that goodbye sex?

"No, no, no." He steps over to me and touches my shoulder to pivot me toward him. "I just wanted to give you something. It's just… a show of good faith. Your payment in advance. You swore your allegiance to me. I wanted to reciprocate."

What the F? I'm still hella confused. I know I usually love money and I always thought having a guy shower me with it would be the ultimate turn-on, but in this instance, I'm totally offended.

My allegiance? I wasn't being loyal for the money. I'm loyal because I care about this family. These two men. And the money was supposed to be mine for doing the job, regardless of my loyalties.

But I do understand that my declaration of loyalty means something to him. Something big. And he's feeling grateful. Which explains the awesome sex.

"Fine, money was the wrong thing." He literally sweeps his hand over the bed and knocks the stacks of cash to the floor like they're nothing. "How about this?" He wraps his arms around me from behind, pulling my back against his front. "I've got every P.I. in the state looking for your little boy. I put them on it as soon as I found out. I promise I'll get him back to you safe and sound."

My knees buckle, the room swoops. "Wh-what?" my voice wobbles. I turn in his arms to see his face. He nods, solemnly.

All I can do is throw my arms around his neck, strangle him with the intensity of my gratitude. And then I'm crying—my tears wetting his neck, my mascara smudging all over his white collar.

"Thank you," I whisper.

He runs his hands up and down my back and I feel so safe. So cared for. Cherished, even. It's an amazing feeling —one I haven't had with a man before.

He cradles one side of my face and thumbs away my tears.

"I still get the money, though, right?" I attempt a joke to lighten the mood.

His smile is devastatingly warm and I bask in its glow. "Of course you do."

"You're awfully sweet for a mob boss," I tell him.

Something in his face shutters—the self-loathing part, I would have to guess. "You're the only person in the entire universe who thinks that."

And I remember how edgy he is with his brothers and sister. How they all act like he's an alligator about to bite them.

I changed him.

It's a stupid and dangerous thought, but I love the feeling that accompanies it.

He's a different man with me.

I think it must be true. Either that, or no one's ever given him credit for his hidden softness. No one's bothered to look at him and see it.

Either way, it makes me even more loyal. Ready to defend him. On his side.

In love.

Crap. I cannot be in love with a mafia kingpin.

I cannot.

But I am.

~

JUNIOR

GIO CONTINUED to improve over the afternoon. While Desiree feeds him some of the salty soup, I order food in for the two of us.

When it arrives, we eat in my living room while we watch *The Bourne Ultimatum* on TV. It's so normal, so comfortable, I have to keep reminding myself not to get used to this.

Later, I catch Desiree after she finishes with her check-in on Gio. I sneak up behind her and wrap one hand around her mouth, the other around her waist.

She screams into my palm.

"Time for your punishment, doll," I growl in her ear as I drag her backward, out of the room.

Her feet scramble to keep up with my lead and I fill my nostrils with her scent. Her silky hair smells fresh and clean like apples, the ponytail slides across my neck as we move.

Once we're in my room I stop and untie the drawstring on her scrub pants, letting them drop to the floor.

The top comes off next and then I spin her around to face me. She's wearing a burgundy satin and lace bra and panty set today. I growl my approval, reaching around to grab her ass and squeeze.

"You always matchy-matchy with your bra and panties?"

"Well, I packed my best," she admits.

Heady satisfaction shoots through me at that. "For me?" I rumble.

"I guess. Yeah." She reaches for the buttons on my shirt but I catch her hands in one of mine.

"Uh uh. I'm in charge." I snag her panties in the back and pull up, flossing them between her ass crack. She goes up on her toes, falling into me. With my free hand, I slap one of her ass cheeks. "You broke the rules again, baby." I gently tug and release the panties, rubbing the taut fabric against her anus and over her clit. "You know what that means?"

"What?" Her breathy voice goes straight to my dick.

"It means you're going to get your beautiful ass fucked."

Her thighs snap together, ass cheeks squeeze up tight at the same time her breath hitches.

I nip her ear as I grip her ass with both hands, kneading the tightened muscles. "You'd better practice relaxing all this, baby. The more your resist me, the harder it will go for you."

Her cheeks relax, first one, then the other.

"That's good," I murmur as I unhook the back of her bra. "Do what you're told and I just might let you come when I'm finished."

Her head snaps up, eyes blazing with her customary defiance. I smile and touch her nose. "I'm gonna start by painting your ass red."

Her pupils are already dilated, breath short. I sit on the bed and tug her over my lap.

"And I thought I'd do it the old fashioned way." I slap her ass.

She makes a surprised little shriek.

I rub the spot I slapped, then tug her panties down and off her legs. "Your ass looks so good with my handprints, baby."

Desiree makes an unintelligible sound. Good, she's already starting on her sexy little noises. I intend to make tonight good for her even if it does push her boundaries. I already tossed a tube of lube on the bed and intend to use plenty. I may call it punishment, but I want it to be the best possible kind.

I give her a spanking. It's more satisfying than I might have guessed—having her bent over my knee like this is real punishment and not just searing sex play. Maybe there is a thread of real discipline in there. Paying her back for making me sweat this morning, for believing she'd betrayed my trust before she turned my world on end by swearing loyalty.

I love this woman.

Fuck, that's crazy to admit, but like my youngest brothers, I'm suddenly a changed man.

Because of a woman.

And her surrender to me—the way she squirms over my lap while I turn her ass pink—is a level of intimacy I never had with anyone—including my...wife. Fuck, I have to tie up that loose end. I can't have a wife when I feel this way about Desiree. Even if I haven't touched Marne in years.

I stop spanking and circle my palm over Desiree's heated skin. She moans softly. More like a hum or a purr. That's it—she's purring. I slide my fingers between her legs, and I'm not surprised when I find she's sopping wet. Her flesh is slick and swollen, welcoming to my touch. Two fingers slide in her easily, gliding in and out. I reach for the bottle of lube with my other hand and pop it open with my thumb.

"You ready for your ass-fucking, baby?" I pry her cheeks apart with the fingers of one hand and squirt a dollop of lube over her asshole.

"No," she says, a sullen teenager tone to her voice. It's so fucking cute I want to kiss her senseless, but instead I pop her ass.

"Wrong answer, doll." I go in immediately, massaging her anus, applying gentle pressure until she relaxes and lets my finger in. Her vocalizations go wild the minute I penetrate her ass, raising in pitch, never stopping. I use my finger to stretch her, get her used to the sensation of having something in her ass. "That's it, baby. Submit. This is the ass-fucking you've been begging for since the minute you got here."

Her pussy drips moisture, moans grow louder.

I pull my finger out and slap her ass. "Bend over the bed, baby." I slide her off my lap and arrange her so her butt is out and ready for me. "If you take my cock like a good girl, I'll let you touch yourself while I punish you."

She doesn't wait for permission. At the suggestion, she

immediately slides her hand between her legs and starts working her slick folds, which makes my aching cock even harder.

I unzip my pants and free my erection, then lube it up good. Pushing her cheeks apart, I line the head up with her anus. "Take it," I tell her, pushing without any force.

She draws in a breath, then lets it out, and the tight muscles yawn to let me in. I ease in slowly, stretching her wide, filling her.

I sense her fingers working frantically between her legs, giving her clit the stimulation she requires to make this pleasure and not discomfort.

"Is this how you thought it would go, doll? In those fantasies of yours?"

"Yes," she moans. "Junior, please."

I'm shaking from holding back. Cristo, I want to pound into her until she screams, but I know better. I go ever-so-slowly, straight in, back out, taking care not to over stretch her. "What do you need, baby? You want it harder?"

"No!" she yelps. "Yes. Wait, I don't know."

I chuckle. "Don't worry, doll. I'm gonna take care of you. I know just how you need to be fucked tonight, and I'm gonna give it to you right. You like having your ass fucked by me?"

She whimpers.

"Hmm?"

"Yes—I don't know. *Please.*"

"Please let you come? Not until I do. You know the rules. This ass belongs to me tonight, and I'm going to fuck it good before I let you get off. *Capiche?*"

"*Capito, capito, capito.* Junior. Ohmygod. Junior. What are you doing to me? Jesus, that's good. That's so good. So crazy. Oh wait, it's too much. It's too much. Wait, please. More. Oh God. *Junior.*"

I let the wave of Desiree-sex-babble roll over me, another hit of pleasure to my senses. The sound of my woman about to combust.

I hold her hips and increase my rhythm, still careful not to get rough or erratic with my thrusts. "You sorry now, baby? Good and sorry?"

"Ohmygod, Junior, I'm so fucking sorry. Please, please, please let me come. I have to come. I need to come right now. Oh please, Junior, please finish. I need more. I need it to be over. I need it so bad."

If I had fewer scruples, I would record her sex babble to re-listen at my leisure. It's like a fucking siren's song, making me crazy with need.

My fingers dig into her hips and I slap against her ass on my way in. I stay in close and bump-bump-bump in and out while she howls with need.

Fuck, I'm going to come. Before I even know it, I'm there. I push in and stay, coming in her ass as I run my hands up and down her back in the sudden release of pleasure.

Not sure if she came, I thrust my hand under her hips to help her, penetrating her pussy and grinding the heel of my hand over her clit. "Come, baby."

"It's too much," she wails, but she does come, her anus tightening with her pussy, drawing an aftershock of release out of me.

"That's it, baby," I croon. I keep moving my fingers

inside her until she relaxes, a limp doll beneath me. Then I work to extricate my body from hers. "Come here, angel." I tug her hips to pull her to her feet.

She moves like she's drugged, all loose-limbed and floppy.

"I'm gonna get you cleaned up in the shower," I murmur, and pick her up in a cradle hold, carrying her into my bathroom.

∼

Desiree

I can barely hold my head up. Junior stands under the warm spray of water with me, his hands roaming over every inch of my body, sudsing and washing and re-sudsing. I'm propped against the wall, smiling at him through the droplets.

I've never seen this face on him. His gaze is pure warmth, so unlike his usual hardened visage, I hardly recognize him. And the warmth is so complete, I could bask in it like the sun. I feel loved and appreciated—cherished even.

Junior shampoos and conditions my hair and when he's done everything but shave my legs, he cages me between his muscled arms and stares down at me, brushing our noses together. "You okay?" He slides one hand down and palms my ass. "Not too sore?"

I shake my head. I'm still one hundred percent blissed out.

He pushes a few strands of wet hair from my face and cups my cheek. "You're good?"

I nod. I guess I used up all my words during sex. Lord, I'm like a non-stop talking sex doll—wind me up and I'll moan and narrate through the whole damn thing.

"What can I do for you?" Junior asks, like he didn't just carry my heavy butt in here and dote on me like a princess. Like he hasn't already done the one thing that matters most—use his power to help me get Jasper back. Or the little things like keeping my favorite ice cream stocked in his freezer.

I shake my head. "Nothing. You've done it."

He keeps studying me, like I might reveal some hidden need. When the water starts to turn cool, he shuts it off and grabs a towel for me first, then for him.

"You'll sleep in my bed," he says.

"Is that an order?" I tease, because in typical Junior fashion, he left out the part about asking me. Or saying please.

His lips twist into a half smile. "You want me to say please? Need me to beg?" Then he shakes his head. "Fuck that. You're sleeping in my bed and that's final."

I laugh because it's totally ridiculous and totally Junior. "You're the boss," I say softly and he smiles.

"Damn right, I am. And you'd better not forget it." He helps me step out of the shower and leads me by the hand to the bed where he pulls the towel off me and watches me climb naked into his bed.

Then he drops his towel and follows me in.

CHAPTER 12

*D*esiree

I WAKE up in Junior's arms. It's an incredible feeling. The brush of his soft chest hair against my cheek, the faint scent of his fading cologne along with the addictive scent of his skin.

I kind of can't believe he's the type to hold a woman all night long, but here we are. My leg tossed over his hips, his cock lined up ready to go between my legs. The moment I stir, his cock bobs, morning wood activated and ready to go.

I reach between us and grip his cock for a squeeze. It swells against my leg, nudging my entrance.

"*Cristo*, baby. You'd better be ready for the monster you're awakening."

I giggle and slip out of bed to run to the bathroom.

"You'd better be coming back to bed," he yells after me.

"Or what?" I call back. I use the toilet and rinse my mouth out with the mouthwash on his counter. He passes me on my way out. "Get back in that bed, or there will be hell to pay."

"Hmm, this is a tough call," I say as I saunter toward the bed. I want to go back to bed, but I also like when there's hell to pay.

Junior laughs from the bathroom. When he comes out, he has a handful of condoms in his fist.

I hold up my finger and thumb like I'm measuring something. "A little hell?"

"I'll give you hell, *bambina.*"

Bambina. That's cute. Is that where they got the name for Bambi?

Junior pulls my legs up by the ankles and slaps my ass a dozen times. *Way* too hard. I scream and yelp and squirm.

"Mac and cheese! Peanut butter. What the hell was my safe word?" I giggle.

Junior drops my ankles, laughter dancing in his affectionate gaze. "Was that enough hell?" he rumbles, low and seductive.

I nod, eyes focused on his face, drinking him in. My dark, handsome lover. Dangerous, wonderful.

Perfect.

He climbs over me and knees open my thighs, then rolls a condom over his fully erect dick. "You sore today?" He rubs his thumb over my slit.

I'm already sopping wet. I swear my sex drive has multiplied by twelve since I came to this house. I know they say a woman's sex drive increases with age, and I'm in my early thirties now, but until this week, it was minimal.

Now? I'm ready every time I hear Junior's deep rumble. Or see the strong lines of his face.

I nod. "Sore in a good way," I tell him. I'm tender between my legs and deep inside, because he's so long he bumped my cervix.

He leans down and plants a kiss at the apex of my labia, over my clit. It's chaste and sweet and not enough. But then he follows it up with a flick of his tongue. A suck. A nip. Then my lips are splayed open by his thumbs and he's going to town on me.

I shriek and jerk, my pussy clenching and releasing, my thighs shivering.

"P-please, Junior." I'm already begging.

"Oh you don't have to beg, angel. I'm definitely going to give it to you."

"N-now?" I moan. Yes. I'm that desperate for his cock. The need to be filled by him is ever-present. Cunnilingus is awesome but not enough.

He sucks hard on my clit, then raises his head, his lips glossy with my juices. "Patience isn't my strong suit, either, doll." He slaps my pussy lightly and climbs over me, his sheathed cock bumping my entrance, homing in on where it belongs.

"F-fuck me." I sound so wanton.

Junior's grin is smug. He eases in gently, which I'm grateful for. I guess I am still pretty sore even though it also feels amazing. He's watching my face closely, like he's looking for signs of distress. "You okay?"

I nod, unable to look away from his warm gaze. I'm

basking in it. Drowning in it. The connection between us is unbelievable. I've definitely never had this with anyone before.

He rocks into me, filling me, stroking my insides, satisfying my need to be possessed by him. We never break eye contact. I rock my hips up to meet his in a dance we both know. A rhythm we share. It's more sensual than sexual. It's not the hot, frenzied need of yesterday. But something deeper. Sweeter. More significant.

"Desiree, I'd do anything for you, baby."

I reach for him, stroke the bulging muscles of his arms, his shoulders, his chest. I flick my fingernails over his taut nipples. "I know," I whisper.

Because I do. I'm sure this man would kill for me. Break the law for me. Protect me with his life. I try not to listen to the voice in my head that tells me a man like him is far too dangerous to love.

"I'm sorry I pulled you into all this."

My chest expands and twists. The apology he owes me. At last. Of course it comes when I no longer need it. Have already forgiven him. Hell, I forgave him that first night when he watched me eat ice cream like I was the most beautiful thing on Earth. But I have a feeling apologizing is an unusual occurrence for him. Same as using please and thank you. So I receive the moment, treasure it as another gift he's given me.

"Apology accepted," I murmur, reaching for his face, wanting to pull him down for a kiss.

He shifts to rest his weight on his hand beyond my shoulder, but doesn't give me the kiss. Instead, he cradles my face, his touch infinitely gentle, even as his thrusts grow harder. "Except if I had to do it again, I'd do the same thing. I wouldn't want to miss this."

My chest splits open—bursts because my heart swelled too big for it. I blink back tears. "Me neither," I admit.

It's the truth. I may not like that I've fallen in love with a mobster, but I have. And I'd do it again.

Junior closes his eyes, like what's between us is too much for him, too. When his eyes open, he picks up speed with his thrusts, all the while keeping his fingers on my face, in a gentle exploration of my cheek, my lips, the side of my neck.

"I don't want it to end," he rasps.

I can't tell if he means the sex or us.

I don't want them to end, either.

But of course, everything must end. It's one of those truths of living you can't fight. Can't ever defeat.

He comes.

I come.

It ends.

And we'll probably end, too.

We need to end, too.

But for now, we can just pretend that ending isn't coming.

∼

"*Cazzo*." Junior pulls out.

"What?" I lean up on my elbows to see what he's cursing about.

"The condom came off. Shit, baby, I'm so sorry."

"Jesus, what are the chances? That was the calmest sex we've had."

He screws up his face in a wry grin—it's sweet and innocent and for a second I think I have a flash of what he must've looked like as a youth. "Let me fish it out. Maybe it still caught most of my cum?"

In the least sexy moment of our relationship, Junior slides his fingers in me to locate the missing condom.

He curses again in Italian as he pulls it out.

There's weight on his shoulders as he walks to the trash and throws it away. When he comes back, his face is ancient again. "We'll get you the morning-after pill. I'm sorry this happened."

Another apology. I could get used to the sweet side of Junior.

I'm still blissed out from the orgasm—no, from more than the orgasm, from the intimacy and sharing we just had, so it takes me a few moments to process what he said.

"No morning-after pill," I say, rolling up out of bed.

"Desiree…" My name sounds so heavy on his lips. Like he's exhausted from years of fighting.

"Seriously, Junior." I'm not willing to block a pregnancy. Not when my heart bleeds for my baby. Not when I consider how much joy that little boy has brought me. "If it's meant to be, it's meant to be," I tell him, even though logic says I should think this through. Having Junior Tacone's child would tie us together for life. And what if it pulled my child into the life he hates? I couldn't allow that.

But still...I wasn't through having children. I just knew better than to have another one with Abe.

Junior turns to face me and pushes his fingers through his hair, making it stick up in all directions. "Baby..." Again, he sounds so tired. "I can't. I really can't."

I turn away from him and pick up my clothes from the floor. "It's not your decision. My body. My choice. End of discussion."

"Desiree." He reaches for me, but seems to change his mind, and instead lunges to block my exit to the bathroom.

I steel myself, chin lifted, nostrils flaring.

He holds his palms up in surrender, but I see equal determination in the set of his jaw, the firm line of his lips. "I can't, Desiree. I'm serious."

"Why not?" I demand. I'm getting mad now. "Because you're still married?"

"No—fuck no. Not that." His throat bobs like he's working to swallow. Turmoil burns behind his eyes. "I...I had a child." His voice sounds strangled. I suddenly sense his pain like a tidal wave bowling both of us over.

My breath leaves my chest, mouth drops open. "Y-you did?" My voice comes out a mere whisper.

He nods, blinking rapidly. "Her name was Mia."

Was.

Oh God. He lost a child. It's the worse thing I can ever imagine.

I'm crying before he can even get the next word out.

"She drowned in our backyard pool. My wife went in to answer the phone and she fell in and—" His words choke off.

I lunge for him, wrap my arms tight around his waist. "I'm so sorry," I sob. "That's so awful. I'm so sorry."

He draws in a ragged breath. "She was three. Sweetest little girl on Earth. Blonde curls and a happy little voice that never stopped chattering." His voice breaks. Restarts. Chokes.

I rub his back like he rubbed mine last night. Press my cheek against his chest, hard. Like I can somehow sink into his chest and take the pain right out of his heart.

His arms are so tight around me, I can't breathe, and I don't care. It's exactly what I want.

"That's why your wife is depressed," I realize aloud.

"Yeah."

"That's why you won't divorce her."

"Yeah."

My heart bleeds for these two ruined people, broken by the death of their tot. I can't imagine anything more horrific.

And now I know why Junior could handle my pain. Why he wasn't afraid of my tears or my mourning on Jasper's birthday. He's been through something far worse. And he still hasn't come out the other side of it.

And just when I don't think I could be any more shocked, feel any deeper range of emotion, Junior says gruffly, "I love you, Desiree."

"Junior," I weep. "I didn't want to fall in love with you. But you're making it so hard."

He eases me away and lifts my chin, a sad smile on his face. "It's okay. I'm not asking for that. I just wanted you to understand. Why I couldn't...I can't."

I nod, but if anything, my resolve is stronger. I believe

in free will, but I also believe in a higher power. I believe I could choose against a pregnancy if I didn't want it. No harm done. That soul would find another place to land. But I also believe that sometimes things are meant to be. Babies can be gifts. To both the mother and the father. What if the events of today resulted in a miracle that changed all our lives for the better?

It's possible.

And I'm willing to allow the cards to fall where they may.

I grip the sides of Junior's face and rise up on my tiptoes to kiss his lips.

And because I don't know what else to say, I just kiss him again. And then I turn and get in the shower.

∼

Junior

I CAN'T BELIEVE I told her about Mia.

I can't believe I said I love you.

But it's the truth. And no other words expressed how I felt in the moment.

Desiree crying real tears for my pain. I love her so much it hurts.

And yet she takes away my pain, too. Because just telling her about Mia—sharing that wound—makes it a little easier.

Yeah, it opened it up again, for sure.

But it also eased some of the pressure.

I listen to the sound of the shower running, and just think about Desiree in there. The most amazing, big-hearted woman on the planet.

I don't deserve her.

Which is why I'm not going to get the girl in this scenario.

She may be falling in love with me, but she doesn't want to be. I need to listen to what she said.

But nothing's going to stop me from taking care of her. Making sure she finds her boy and gets her happily ever after even if it's without me.

I pull on some boxer briefs and an undershirt and check on Gio. I'm relieved to find his fever's gone. He blinks his eyes open and looks at me. "Hey, *fratello*."

"How're you feeling, Gio?"

"Good. Better. Where's your little nurse?"

"In the shower."

Gio nods. "You're gonna keep her after all this, right?"

The heaviness I've been trying to resist descends. "Not gonna happen. And mind your own fucking business."

"Seriously, Junior? She's *great*." He emphasizes great, like I might've missed how fucking amazing she is.

"Yeah, she is. And she wants no part of *La nostra*. So I gotta let her go."

Gio stares at me. "*Fanculo*. You really love this girl, don't you?"

"Shut up, Gio," I say, but there's no venom behind the words. I only feel tired.

Tired and defeated. Because the woman I love is going to walk out of the house within days.

And I may never see her again.

CHAPTER 13

Desiree

"There's a man involved. I know there's a man involved." My coworker and friend Lucy bumps my hip with hers. I've been back at work for two days, still staying at Junior's place at night to check on Gio. And have hot sex.

I took Gio's IV out, and he's just in rest and recuperate mode—sitting up, watching television, eating and drinking normally. His recovery looks good.

It feels weird to be back at the hospital—like I was gone for a month instead of just a week. Lucy's been asking a million questions about my mystery job.

Because, yeah. I'm not ready for this tryst to be over.

"How do you know?" I laugh.

"I can just tell. You have that freshly-laid look. Like you've been getting some. And more than just once."

I grin.

"Seriously, you can tell when a woman starts having a lot of sex. Her skin gets brighter, her mood is lighter. It's the release of nitric oxide."

"Oh really?" I give her a doubtful look.

"Look it up. It's true."

"Okay, yes, there's a man involved. But it's a fling. Nothing permanent or serious," I say firmly, like I'm willing myself to believe it.

"We'll see," Lucy sings as a patient's buzzer rings and she scurries off.

I smile after her, feeling all warm and glowy when I really shouldn't. But it's been fun, coming into work and then going "home" to Junior.

Submitting to his unrestrained sexual demands and receiving everything in return. He insists on dropping me off and picking me up from work.

I should see it as controlling, but instead I feel loved.

Like he can't stand to be away for even the extra thirty minutes it would take me to drive myself. Or like he's so protective he doesn't want me walking in the parking lot alone. He actually voiced the latter to me even though I told him the only jerks waiting in the parking lot belong to him.

"Desiree." His deep voice cuts through my thoughts as if he's actually here.

Oh shit, he's actually here! And I still have four hours left on my shift.

"Junior, what are you doing here?" I glance around, hoping my boss is nowhere near. I do not need to get busted for this, especially after being "out sick" for a full week.

He looks stony serious. It's the look he used to always wear, but I'd forgotten it in the past few days. "Desiree, get your shit, we need to go."

I frown. "Junior, I can't. I'm working. What is it? Is it Gio?" His brother's been doing so well, I'd be shocked to hear he's had another relapse.

He shakes his head. "It's Jasper. I know where he is. Come on, let's go get him."

My heart shifts into highest gear. "Oh my God, are you serious? Where?"

"Indiana. Come on, we can make it by five if we leave now."

"I'll be right back," I say, already dashing off to find my boss. I know she's going to flip out with my absenteeism, but this can't wait. At least she already knows about my personal problems. I burst into tears telling her and she hugs me. "Go. Personal emergency. I'll find someone to come in." She shoos me away. "Bring that baby back home."

"I will," I promise, still weeping. I run back down the hall to where Junior's waiting for me and take his hand.

And then my brain just sort of shuts off. Because I can't wait the five hours until we get there. And I can't think about anything else.

Fortunately, Junior seems to understand. Is totally capable in this situation. He drives the Maserati like we're in the Daytona 500 and gets us the hell out of Illinois.

∽

Junior

. . .

Desiree's ex picked up a construction job in Indianapolis under some other guy's social security number. I don't know how the P.I.s found him, but they did. Jasper seems to be fine—enrolled in kindergarten. Stays for aftercare. Gets picked up and dropped off on the regular. No signs of mistreatment.

Thank fuck.

And I'm still going to kill the *figlio di puttana* father.

No, not kill. Desiree doesn't want that. But I'm sure as hell gonna teach him a fucking lesson. Nobody messes with someone I care about without serious consequences.

My plan is to get to the school before Jasper gets picked up, but we get hung up in traffic on the way out of the city, so I don't think we'll get there before five.

On the way, my phone rings. It's Nico.

"Hey, little bro."

"Not little," he claims.

"That's not what your wife says."

If he were talking to one of our other brothers, he'd tell me where to fuck myself, but as oldest, I've always demanded the same respect from my brothers they give our pops, so he just grunts.

"You're on speaker and Desiree's in the car," I warn, in case he was going to talk business. We're careful about what we say on phones, anyway, but it's worth telling him.

"Hi, Desiree."

"Hi." She turns to me and whispers, "Which brother is it?"

"It's Nico," I tell her.

"Yeah, Nico. Sorry. I just talked to Gio. He sounds good."

"Yes, looks like he'll make a—"

"Not over the phone," I cut her off.

She snaps her lips shut. "Right."

"What's up?" I bark at Nico. It's not like him to call to chit-chat.

"Listen, I uh, have some news."

"What news?" I'm already grouchy. I don't like news. It's never good. And Nico sounds nervous to tell me.

"Sondra and I are, uh...well, she's pregnant."

My stomach draws up under my ribs into a tight knot. I can't breathe. This is good news. This should be good news he's telling me.

Why does it feel like I just got sucker-punched?

"Oh yeah?" I force myself to speak. "Congratulations. How far along?"

"About twelve weeks."

"Twelve weeks. Wow, you waited to tell people, uh?"

"Yeah. Well, Stefano knew, but we're just telling the rest of the family now. I don't know if it's hard for you—"

"Shut up, Nico." I cut him off, angry by his suggestion, even though it's spot on. Maybe because it's spot on. "Go give your wife a kiss from me. On the cheek, of course. Tell her congratulations and I can't wait to meet my new niece or nephew, uh?"

"Okay, I'll do that." Nico sounds relieved. The fucker was worried about calling me. I don't know why that pisses me off, too. Like people expect me to implode over a new baby in the family.

Just because I lost the only one this family's had. You'd

think out of five siblings, my ma would be wading in grandchildren, but to her sorrow, that hasn't been the case.

"*Congratulazioni*, Nico. Ma's gonna be over the moon."

"Yeah, I know. You wanna tell Dad?"

"No, tell him yourself."

"He still pissed at me?"

"If he was pissed, you'd know it. Have you not talked to him since you got married?" Last year Nico defied our father's order to marry a girl from the Pachino family in a contract that was meant to tie the families and businesses together. It was my job to teach him a lesson for his disobedience.

Which kept me solidly in the position of most hated brother.

"No."

"Call him up. All is forgiven. You paid the price, and it's settled. I'm sorry you didn't know that."

"Yeah, well, things get lost in translation between the two of you sometimes."

"Yeah and you're pushing your luck, *stronzo*. You already got an apology out of me. Mark it on the calendar so we can remember this day in history."

A surprised laugh comes out of Nico. I almost smile myself. It's unheard of—me, making fun of myself.

Desiree slides a glance my way and her lips quirk, too. Her gaze is soft and warm, like she knows everything the conversation means to me and is sending me her support. This woman is something else.

As Nico hangs up, I reach over and squeeze her knee in a silent thank you.

Desiree

My stomach twists in knots the whole drive, hands ice cold. First, I couldn't think at all, but as we pull into Indianapolis, a million thoughts swirl through my head. The major underlying anxiety runs along the lines of—what if he's not there? What if we haven't really found him? Or can't take him when we get there?

"I was hoping we'd get here before Jasper gets picked up from the after school program at five," Junior says.

I tilt my head, replaying his words in my mind, because my brain isn't working straight.

He must see that I don't understand, because he explains, "I don't know, I thought it might be easier on him if you picked him up instead of his dad. And then we just drove off. But the school might not have released him." Junior shakes his head. "It's probably gonna be messy, no matter what."

My eyes prick with tears of gratitude. I can't believe how much thought he's put into this—his consideration for Jasper. Junior may come off as a tough-guy meathead, but he's way more. He's nuanced. Sophisticated.

I remember how he slipped the girl in the cafe the money. It made me jealous—which was stupid—but part of my jealousy was over the thought and effort he put into the gesture.

He pulls up in front of a brick house. "This is it. That's

Abe's truck." He points to an old Ford F150 parked in front of us. "Abe rents the basement."

He parks the car and pulls a gun out of a holster next to his seat.

My brain finally kicks into gear. "Whoa, whoa, whoa. What are you doing?"

He pauses but raises his brows like he doesn't understand the question.

"You're not bringing a gun in there." I point toward the house. "My six-year-old kid is in there. And Abe is his father."

Junior sighs.

"No. Guns," I say firmly.

A new set of fears suddenly comes crashing around me. Junior and Abe. This isn't going to go well. That's part of why he thought picking Jasper up from school would be better. Junior is one hundred percent alpha male, which means he's going to have to piss all over Abe.

Not that Abe doesn't deserve it, but things could get messy here, really fast. And I don't need messy. I just want to get my son and get out of here.

I want to either burst into tears or puke as we walk up the sidewalk, then down the steps to the basement door. Junior's expression is hard, eyes dead. A shiver runs down my spine. "Maybe you should wait in the car," I tell him when we get to the door.

He goes still, studying me, then draws back a half a step and angles his back against the brick wall. "I'll be right here," he says, folding his arms over his chest.

His position as bodyguard reassures me. I draw a deep breath and knock on the door.

Abe's stupid enough to swing the door wide without looking out the peephole first. When he gets over his surprise at seeing me, he tries to shut it again, but I launch myself through the doorway. He slams the door back, and clocks me in the head and shoulder.

My vision bleeds black as pain explodes at the points of impact.

Junior surges into motion like a dark, avenging angel. I'm still seeing stars as he kicks the door open like we're in a movie, simultaneously propelling me into the basement apartment.

"Mommy!" Jasper yells and then I really can't see, because my vision goes blurry with tears.

Jasper and I both cry, strangling each other with hugs. It takes me a minute to realize how bad the situation got. Just feet from us, Junior's brawling with Abe.

No, make that beating the shit out of Abe. The crack of bone on bone splits the air and Abe's body flies past us, crashing into the coffee table with a sickening thud.

Jasper screams.

Abe groans, but tries to get up.

Junior stalks over, picks him up by his shirt and punches his bloody face.

"Junior."

Junior ignores me, punching Abe again and again.

"Junior!" I scream.

I don't want Jasper to see this. Any of it.

I also don't want to put him down or out of my sight, even for a second. Ever again. But I need to stop Junior before he kills Abe.

I scream his name again, then body check him with my shoulder, my son still wrapped up tight in my arms.

When he glances at me, his expression chills me to the bone. There's nothing there. No life at all. He's cold. Deadly. Dangerous.

He must see the fear in my face, though, because the horrifying mask disintegrates, and then he's the Junior I know. His brows drop, forehead wrinkles in concern.

I realize I'm still bawling. "Junior, no," I beg. "Stop this. Right now."

He looks at Abe who can barely move on the floor, then back at me and his expression clouds, like he realizes what he's done. "*Fanculo*," he mutters, scrubbing a hand over his face. His knuckles are swollen and bloody.

Abe can't seem to get up. Jesus, Junior did some damage. What if he'd brought the gun in?

Ice sluices through my veins.

I know what would've happened.

My son's father would be dead right now.

How far from reality did I drift that I thought bringing a violent mobster on the most important errand of my life with me would end well? And now, as if Jasper hasn't been traumatized enough by his kidnapping, he will be forever scarred by seeing his father brutally assaulted by his mother's boyfriend.

Not okay.

Not in any realm or reality.

I fish my phone out of my purse. I need to take charge of this situation and do what's right. "I'm calling an ambulance," I mutter.

"Don't," Junior warns.

"You don't get to make this decision," I snarl at him.

The color drains from his face. He takes a step back and his eyes go dead again.

I carry Jasper into his bedroom while I make the 911 call, then hang up and set him down. "You're coming home with Mommy now. I missed you so much, Jasper." I drop to my knees and give him another bear hug.

"I missed you, too, Mommy." His little voice kills me. So sweet. So precious to my ears.

"What do you want to pack to bring along? Any special toys or stuffed animals?" He has a favorite pillow he was terribly attached to at home. I cried into it at least a dozen times, wondering how he was sleeping without it.

"I'll bring Mr. Dragon." He picks up a rainbow-colored stuffed dragon.

"Anything else?"

He shakes his head. "I just want to go home."

Ugh. I moved after his dad took him from me because I needed to downgrade to afford the P.I. I'm not going to tell Jasper that now, though.

I pick him up again and carry him into the living room as the sirens approach the house.

Junior's standing in the open door, waiting for the swarm of cops and paramedics who stream into the little apartment.

As the second shit-storm of the night rolls in, I realize I probably made a huge mistake.

∽

Junior

. . .

THE COPS throw me face down and cuff me as soon as they arrive, even though I offer no resistance. I expected this kind of treatment, though. I just didn't want Desiree or her boy to have to see it.

Cristo, I fucked up.

Big time.

I already wanted to throttle her *stronzo* ex for what he put her through taking the boy, but when I saw him smash the door into her face, I relished killing him.

But not in front of her. Not in front of the boy. I should've pulled back. Or pulled him out of the apartment. I don't know. I should've done something different.

Because now I'm sure I've lost Desiree. The horror and condemnation on her face make it clear.

"Well, look here," one of the two beat cops who showed up drawls. "Driver's license says this is Santo Tacone, from Chicago. Wouldn't be related to the Don Tacone sitting in a Federal Prison right now, wouldya?"

I don't answer.

It earns me a swift kick to the ribs. Fine. Local cops want to be heroes and give me a beat-down, they're welcome to it. I probably deserve it for what I'm putting Desiree through.

After a few more bruising kicks, the other cop, who was interviewing Desiree, snaps, "What the fuck are you doing?"

"He was resisting arrest," the first cop says.

"You got a room full of witnesses, dumbshit," he says, which is true. The tiny apartment also has three paramedics in it, as well as Desiree and Jasper. "And seriously—I don't think you wanna fuck with this guy." He hooks an arm under mine and tugs, helping me off the floor and to my feet.

"Are you kidding? We got Santo Tacone, Jr. on something solid. Assault and battery. No way we're not taking this as far as we can."

"Let him go," Desiree storms. "He was just protecting me." I'm more than a little relieved that she's defending me, although I'm not stupid enough to think it changes things. Clearly she didn't see this coming. She hasn't been on the wrong side of the law her whole life, like I have.

The first cop looks confused.

"It was self-defense." The second cop unlocks my handcuffs.

I have to hide my shock. But this could be the classic Good Cop, Bad Cop play.

"Are you kidding me? He put that guy in the hospital," Bad Cop says.

"So he got a little aggressive. I'd be hot, too, if someone hit my girlfriend and kidnapped her child."

I keep my mouth shut. I know better than to ever say a word in front of law enforcement.

The paramedics wheel Abe out on a stretcher. Good Cop speaks into his radio.

Bad Cop narrows his eyes. "You're scared of this guy. Wait—you're from Chicago, aren't you?"

"I grew up in Tacone territory, yeah. What I remember mostly is they kept the streets safe. So, no. I don't have a hard-on for putting a guy away who was acting hero for his girlfriend."

I give the guy my full attention now, studying him, checking the name on his badge—John Badger.

"Badger Hardware," I say, when the name comes to me. A locally-owned hardware store in Cicero, before Home Depot and Lowes put the small guys out of business. Actually, that store's still there, a throwback to older times.

Good Cop's face splits into a grin. "Yep. That's my uncle's place. It's still around."

"It sure is," I say.

Good Cop's phone rings and he answers it, stepping outside.

Bad Cop glowers at me.

I keep still.

Desiree's pacing around the tiny apartment, still holding Jasper in her arms, picking up his clothes and toys and throwing them in a plastic bag. Every so often I hear her sniff, which completely guts me.

The kid, too, looks traumatized. He has a death grip on his mother's neck, face tucked in like he doesn't want to see any of what's going on.

Good Cop comes back and addresses Desiree. "All right, I have confirmation of your story. Police records in Cook County show you have full custody of Jasper and the father abducted him from you. You are free to take him home."

"Thank you." Desiree glances in my direction without quite looking at me. "What about him?"

"He's free to go, too."

"Are you nuts?" Bad Cop snarls.

Good Cop holds his hand out to me and I shake it,

relieved that for once, my family and my name won me a favor instead of lost it for me.

My dad did some things right.

He operated by a code of ethics, just outside the law. He made his own law.

But this isn't a win, by any means. Desiree turns and walks out the door without ever meeting my eye and I know, without a shadow of a doubt, that we're over.

CHAPTER 14

Desiree

I SLEEP in the back of Junior's car, Jasper curled up in my lap. It's not a peaceful sleep, it's the kind I choose when I can't deal with my thoughts and just need to escape them. I should be overjoyed at having Jasper back.

I am overjoyed.

Or I'm sure I will be tomorrow. But right now, it's all too much emotion mixed together.

I wake up when we get into the city, as if my body was awake and knew where I was the whole time. It's late—almost two in the morning. Jasper's sweet face rests against my chest, his breath easy and soft.

"Junior, I need you to take me to my home," I tell him.

Jasper stirs and I rub the back of his head like I did when he was a baby.

"Yeah." That's all he says. The distance between us is an

ocean. We haven't spoken the entire ride home.

He takes me to my apartment and opens up the door, reaching for Jasper and pulling him out and into his arms as I climb out.

My urge to snatch my baby back is strong, even though I know Junior means him no harm. Maybe it's more that he seems too good at this. Too fatherly. Too familiar.

As if he knows it, he hands him to me the second I get out and reaches in for the plastic bag of Jasper's stuff I collected from Abe's place.

"Junior." My voice sounds strangled and unnatural. "I really appreciate what you did for me—getting Jasper back. It means everything to me." I swallow down the lump in my throat. Tears sting my eyes. "But I just need to be home with him now. So this is goodbye."

Junior's face is the same stony mask he's worn since Indianapolis. It doesn't change. He just nods and walks me up to the building. Takes my keys and opens the door, then leads the way up the stairs to my place and opens that door, too. He sets Jasper's things inside the door, but doesn't cross the threshold.

And then he pulls the door shut.

No touch or word. No goodbye.

Nothing.

It's just... over.

I don't know what I wanted, but I'm suddenly sobbing —heartbroken over the choice I made.

But it was the right one.

The only one I could make.

My world—raising my beautiful little boy—it can't

mix with Junior's world. Not ever again.

Jasper will probably be forever scarred by what he saw back there. He will never forget the night I came for him and my "boyfriend" nearly killed his father.

If I want to raise my son right, I have to walk away from the powerful allure of Junior Tacone. Even if he is my personal hero.

I carry Jasper into my room and lay him on my bed.

My baby's back. That should be enough.

That should definitely be enough.

I'm sure eventually this emptiness, this queasy panic bubbling up inside me will go away.

∼

Junior

Letting Desiree go feels like taking my face to a grater. My entire body revolts. Every mile I drive away from her sends me into a deeper panic.

But I can't go back. I won't try to convince her to be with me.

It's wrong.

As much as I want to go back there, load her and the boy up and tell them they're moving in with me, end of story, I can't.

She needs me out of her life.

After the way I behaved in front of her child, I can't blame her. I would never allow my own child to see such a thing.

And just like that, the pain of losing Mia is so fresh again, it surges to the surface, mingles with the ache of leaving Desiree. Desiree and Jasper.

Because, yes, I care about that boy, too. He's part of Desiree. He's her entire world. I would do anything for him, same as her.

I drive home and drown myself in a bottle of Scotch.

Let her go.

I have to let her go.

Even if it kills me.

∼

"You ever coming out of this office?" Gio pokes his head in my den, where I've been sitting for the past seventy-two hours.

I can't seem to move.

Or speak.

Or do anything.

Paolo called, he's chasing down a lead on Vlad, and he asked me what to do if he finds him. It turns out the guy was in Russia when the meet at Milano went down, so I don't know if Ivan was operating on his own or not. Vlad only just turned up back in town to find his entire operation shut down by me.

The order should be, "kill him."

It's seems pretty plain, right? Vlad sent his men to kill me, so now that I've killed his men, I should hunt him down and kill him.

Except I can't seem to give the order.

Desiree wouldn't like it.

JOKER'S WILD

Hell, I don't even like it. I have no proof that Vlad gave the order. And I have no evidence that Vlad is coming after me, though logic says he would. I should be prepared for an attack. I should go on the offensive and take him out.

But I don't want to.

I don't actually want to do anything.

"Have you eaten? Or slept?" Gio asks. He left my house the day I drove to Indianapolis—his recovery nearly complete. Now he's stopped in without an invite. And without knocking.

Or maybe he knocked and I just ignored it.

"You sure as hell haven't showered." Gio wrinkles his nose.

I want to pull an old Junior and be an asshole so he'll leave, but it's hard for me to be a dick to him. I just keep remembering how it felt to think he might die. Or maybe I just don't want to be that guy anymore.

"You ever think about getting out of the business?" I ask Gio.

"What?" He walks into my office and drops into a chair across from the desk.

"Like Nico and Stefano. Ever want to leave? Or hope they'll need you over there?"

Gio's quiet long enough that I know the answer.

"Why do you stay?"

Gio shrugs. "I'm not going to fucking leave you here to run shit on your own. That's not fair."

I'm floored.

One of my brothers is concerned about being fair *to me*? The biggest dick in the family? All I've ever done is

197

thrown my weight around and demand their absolute loyalty and obedience. There's a hierarchy here, and I make sure they follow it.

My throat closes.

"And someone has to be here to run shit." I say flatly, although it's really a question. Is there any chance we could close up shop?

Hang our hats up and retire? Or move onto something better—whatever the hell that may be?

Gio considers me for another long moment. "Is that true?"

"Pops thinks so."

"Yeah." Gio fiddles with his Rolex. "But what for? He's gonna want to kick it on a beach with Ma when he gets out. He's not going to want this business back."

"It's his legacy."

"The Bellissimo is his fucking legacy. His money, his business—*our* fucking business—started that. Yeah, Nico was smart. Nico leveraged it right. Hit it big. But we can all hang our names on that project. Because we're the ones who risked our fucking lives from the time we were old enough to curl our fingers into a fist to earn that money. We gave up our fucking souls for that money." There's bitterness in Gio's voice.

The same bitterness I feel. The kind that's mingled in with intense loyalty, so it turns inward in shame and crushing darkness.

Would I wish my fate on my own brothers? Have them stay in this business just so I'm not alone?

Hell, no.

I almost lost Gio over this stupid *Cosa Nostra*.

"Let's end it." My throat goes dry as soon as I say it. Shame washes over me. But bigger than the shame, the fear I'm betraying my father, comes relief.

So much relief.

"Yeah?" Gio sounds as shocked as I feel.

"Yeah. Unless Paolo disagrees. We make this unanimous."

Gio cracks a grin. "I thought this wasn't a fucking democracy." He throws the refrain I used to always use back at me.

I can't quite smile back, but I try. "It is now."

"And then what?" Gio asks as he gets up.

I shrug, heaviness descending back on my shoulders. "I have no fucking idea."

"No. Then you go get the girl. 'That's what this is about, right?"

My chest constricts painfully. Not a second has gone by since I drove away from Desiree that I haven't thought about her. Wondered how she's doing. What it's like being reunited with her little boy. Whether she's carrying my child right now.

I shake my head slowly.

"Junior. Don't fuck this up. Or if you already did, then you'd better unfuck it. That girl made you happy. You'd better do whatever it takes to figure it out."

I stare at Gio, not daring to listen to his advice. "But what if my happiness comes at the expense of hers?"

Gio winces a bit as he stands, his hand covering the wound. "Make sure it doesn't." He leaves me with that nugget and a wave.

Make sure it doesn't. Can I?

What would it take to ensure Desiree's happiness? Quitting the business—I'm doing that.

Divorcing Marne—that's long overdue. I pick up the phone and dial my lawyer to draw up the papers. I'll give her half of everything. She'll be better off than she ever was married or separated from me.

~

Desiree

Junior Tacone is stalking me.

It's been three weeks since he dropped me off at my apartment. Three weeks of getting to know my son again, loving him, playing with him, soaking up every second with him. And working my three twelve hour shifts that end at 7:00 p.m.

And every night when I walk out to my car, Junior's black Maserati is parked somewhere in the vicinity. The first night I pretended I didn't see him. I fully expected him to get out and corner me against my car, but he didn't. Nothing happened. I got in my car and drove off, checking in the rear view mirror to see if he followed.

He didn't.

The second night I marched over to his car. "What are you doing here?" I demanded when he rolled down the window.

"Just making sure you get to your car safely. I don't like you walking out here alone at night."

I put my hands on my hips. "Yeah, I did have trouble in

this lot one time." I watched his jaw tighten, expression turn foreboding. "Oh wait, they were your guys, weren't they?"

He leaned back in his seat. "Well, your ex may show up anytime. I'm not here to interfere in your life. I'm just making sure you have back up if you need it."

I stared at him, stunned. Well, if he wanted to play bodyguard, I'd let him. I figured he'd get tired of it soon. Or he'd renege on his promise not to interfere.

But neither of those things have happened yet.

And now I know for certain I'm carrying his baby. I had a blood test today at the hospital.

When Junior finds out, he's going to put his claim on me, just like he's kept his claim on his wife. I have no delusions that he'll stay detached or removed.

And like his wife, I'm not sure I have the resources or the guts to fend him off.

I ignore him as I walk by, like I do every night he's here. And like those nights, he makes no attempt to talk to me or attract my attention.

I get in my car and drive away, fighting the urge to turn around to drive back. Tell him about the baby.

His baby.

Our baby.

If he keeps stalking me like this, he'll find out soon enough. And I doubt I'll be strong enough to keep him away when that happens.

And that thought should be frightening, not reassuring.

CHAPTER 15

Desiree

Another wave of nausea hits me and I heave my breakfast into the toilet.

Thirteen weeks.

Hopefully by the end of next week I'll be past the morning sickness phase.

"Mommy, you okay?" My sweet Jasper asks from the doorway.

"Yep," I say brightly, splashing water on my face and rinsing my mouth out.

"You need someone here to take care of you."

I turn, surprised by this observation. "You're here, aren't you?"

"I mean a man. Where's your boyfriend?"

I go still. "What boyfriend?"

"The man who came with you when you got me from Daddy's." It's the first time Jasper's mentioned Junior. I'm sure I screwed up as a mother, but I never addressed what happened that night. I felt too emotional about breaking up with Junior and I guess I didn't know what to say to Jasper to take away the trauma of what he saw.

"He would take care of you, Mommy. He would keep us safe."

My heart starts to pound. "Safe from what?" My voice cracks.

"From Daddy. Or bad stuff. I think he wants to help us."

"Jasper...how do you know? What makes you say that?"

Jasper shrugs. "I just know. He'd be a good dad to me."

Tears leak from my eyes before I even realize I'm crying them. I have no idea what prompted Jasper to say these things.

Jasper wraps his arms around my waist and hugs me. "It's okay, Mommy. You don't have to be sad any more."

"Aren't you afraid of Junior? After what he did to your daddy?"

Jasper shakes his head. "No."

Just *no*. No other explanation for his take on the situation. I still haven't ferreted out much about Jasper's stay with his dad. I don't think he was mistreated, but he definitely seems relieved to be with me again. The first few weeks he kept asking me if his dad would come and take him again. I promised him he wouldn't, although I'm not sure how I'll keep that promise. Right now he's in jail, and looking at up to a year in prison for taking Jasper. After that, though? Who knows what will happen.

I draw in a shaky breath. "So you think I should let Junior be my boyfriend again?" My voice wobbles on the words. I didn't realize how badly I wanted it until I said it out loud.

"Definitely," Jasper says.

Definitely. Wow. Okay.

∼

JUNIOR

I WAIT for Desiree to round the corner in the parking lot. She's parked in her usual place, and I'm in mine—a spot across from her car.

There's something different about her today. Vulnerability glimmers on her face. She finds me with her gaze, as she always does, but this time she keeps looking. Keeps walking, straight toward my car. I roll down the window, but she walks past without saying anything. Then pulls open the passenger side door and climbs in.

My entire body comes alive at being close to her again. I want to reach for her, to touch her skin, taste her lips, but I utilize the restraint I've been practicing these last few months. Winning Desiree back is going to take time. I had to get my life in order, prove I can be the man she needs me to be.

And I'm getting there.

"Hey," she says softly. She's still wearing the ring I bought her. She never took it off. I try not to read too much into that.

Fuck it, I can't resist any longer. I reach for her hand and pick it up. "Hey," I say back.

"Junior...I'm pregnant."

I squeeze her hand, bringing it to my lips to kiss. "I know, baby."

Her brown eyes widen. "You knew?"

"Yeah, doll. And believe me, it took all my willpower not to just barrel into your place, pack all your shit up and move you and Jasper in with me the second I figured it out."

Tears glisten in her eyes and I go rigid, not sure what they're for. "Why didn't you?" she croaks.

I cradle the side of her face. "Did you want me to?"

She shakes her head and a tear drops down her cheek. "No, not really."

I try to decipher that answer. "Listen, doll. I have some things to tell you."

"Yeah?" she lifts her wet lashes to gaze at my face.

"My brothers and I talked and we're shutting down the family business—retiring. No more danger. No more illegal activities. And I got divorced. It was final this week."

She swallows. "W-was that for me?"

"For you. Only for you. Totally for you. Desiree, I've missed you so goddamn much. I want you in my life. I want to figure out how we can make it work. Because, baby, you changed me. I'm a different man than I was before you came into my house.

"Into my heart. It's like I was living life in black and white before I met you. And then you showed me technicolor. And since you've been gone—I'm not living life at all.

"I've just been working to make myself worthy of you.

"I want you to know if you let me into your life, I will never show my violent side to you or Jasper ever again. I'll never let him see a gun. Or teach him to fight—unless you want me to. I'll take care of you two—and the new one, of course. I have plenty of money. You don't have to work. You can stay home with the kids, if you want. Or I'll stay home with the kids. Because I haven't figured out what I'm going to do with myself, yet."

Desiree lets out a watery laugh.

"Is that a yes?"

"That depends—what am I saying yes to?"

I shrug, afraid to say the wrong thing. I want to ask for it all—moving in together. Marriage. The whole package. "To me?"

She smiles through her tears. "Yes."

For one solid beat, I can't believe my ears. "Yes, you want to be with me?"

She nods happily. "Yes, Junior. So does Jasper. He told me this morning."

I fall back against the seat, humbled. Overwhelmed.

"Well?" Desiree demands.

I raise my brows, not sure what she wants.

"Aren't you going to kiss me?"

Dizzy with relief, maddened by lust, I lunge across the car and capture her face between my hands, pull it to mine. My lips descend over hers, moving, molding, nipping. My tongue sweeps between her lips and then we're both frantic, devouring each other with our kisses.

"I love you, Junior," Desiree whispers when we break apart.

"I love you more, doll."

EPILOGUE

*D*esiree

A HIGH-PITCHED SCREECH of laughter comes out of Jasper's room. I smile, and bite back my admonishment that bedtime is not the time for tickles. Junior's in with my son —our son—reading him *How Do Dinosaurs Say Goodnight* which must've turned into a tickle-fest.

My baby kicks and I rub my belly as I dig my spoon into the carton of Ben & Jerry's Junior always keeps stocked for me. Only a few weeks to go until we can meet our baby—another boy.

I think Junior was relieved not to have a girl—no comparing this one to his little lost angel. Although I'm sure he would've loved a girl with his whole heart, too. He's been amazing with Jasper, who already seems as in love with him as I am.

"All right, he's ready for goodnight kisses from you,"

Junior says, appearing in the doorway. His face is open and alive—so different from how it looked when I first met him. The underlying sense of violence is gone and so is his guardedness. He stops me as I pass for a kiss and I lift my hand to his neck, melting into him.

"I'll see you in the bedroom," Junior rumbles. "You have another punishment coming."

My pussy clenches. As if the pregnancy hormones don't have me horny enough, Junior makes most every night a new adventure in the bedroom. I can hardly look at him without getting wet these days. Although I have to say, with my current shape, it's getting harder and harder to find new positions.

I give Jasper his "bed night kiss" as he calls it, and head up the stairs. Junior hasn't made it up yet, so I get into the shower. I try to resist—I really do—but just thinking about all the dirty things Junior will do and say to me when he arrives have me three strokes from an orgasm. I make the water cooler and lean my forehead against the cool tile, exploring between my legs with one hand. My folds are juicy wet—like always these days. I rub my clit and moan.

"Ahem." Junior clears his throat from the other side of the shower door and I scream. He laughs as he opens the glass door and steps in, naked. "Did I say you could masturbate?"

I whimper, because there's no way I'm tearing my hand away now—it feels too good and I'm about to climax.

"Bad girl." He wraps a fist in my wet hair and tugs my hair back, planting a kiss at the place where shoulder meets neck. His other hand curls over the top of mine, fingers penetrating me, pushing mine in with his.

That's all it takes. I buck as an orgasm rips through me, then my vision goes black and starry because I almost pass out. The increased blood volume from pregnancy has its downsides, for sure.

It doesn't matter, because Junior would never let me fall. He strokes his palms lovingly over my body, exploring every inch, giving so much to me with just the simple caress. I know this sensory appreciation is part of the pregnancy, too. Every nerve ending is primed and sensitive. I can't take much spanking or anything rough— Junior has to make it way more pretend than real for our forced game.

My punishment tonight is over not spending enough money. I kept my job at the hospital—I told him I wanted to work at least until the baby comes. He gave me a credit card when I moved in, but I never use it. I don't know—I don't like spending his money, that makes me feel guilty and wasteful. I'd rather have him spend it on me. So he comes up with games, like he did the first day he took me shopping. I have a certain amount of time in which I have to spend a certain amount or I get punished.

It's so hot. I'm off the hook for being wasteful. In fact, I'm required to be. And I feel spoiled rotten by the end of it. Plus, I often don't quite complete the challenge, so there's the fun in the bedroom afterward.

Today I managed to spend $2,500, mostly on gifts for Jasper and my mom, but I was supposed to spend $3,000.

Junior turns off the water. "I'm going to make you pay for that orgasm, baby."

"Oh yeah?" I'm still dizzy from lust and my orgasm. "How?"

"You're going to be coming all night long, angel. No rest for the wicked. I'm going to fuck you until you cry."

I laugh, because I probably will cry—it doesn't take much these days and he's done it before. And it sounds wonderful to me. Perfect, actually.

I let him towel me off and hold my hand while I step out of the shower. He treats me like I'm the most precious object on Earth, and some days I hardly believe it's real. He leads me to the bedroom. "Bend over for your spanking."

I whimper in advance, because it takes almost nothing these days to make me yelp. I rest on my forearms on the mattress to make room for my belly, and present my backside.

He strokes my ass instead, his large palm traveling in circles around my cheeks. "You don't want a spanking tonight, do you, angel?"

I shake my head.

He drags a finger down my crack, over my anus. "I'll have to punish you a different way, then." He moves away from me to open the dresser drawer where he keeps our sex toys. When he comes back, he drops a vibrator, buttplug and lube beside me on the bed. I let out a wanton moan just from thinking about him using them on me.

He gives my ass a gentle slap, then rubs between my legs. Even though I just orgasmed in the shower, I'm ready for more—it seems to be my perpetual state. Junior pries my cheeks apart and drops a dollop of lube over my back hole. When he brings the tip of the buttplug against the tight ring of muscles, I moan in pleasure.

Gone is my fear of back door sex. Junior initiated me into an entire world of butt stuff, and I'm a total convert now. He teases me with the plug, pushing it in a couple centimeters, then drawing it back out. My pussy quivers with anticipation, with pleasure.

"Junior," I moan.

"Start begging, baby. Lemme hear it."

I wriggle my hand under my hips, needing pussy stimulation. Junior slaps my ass. "Did I say you could touch yourself?"

"Please, Junior. I'm dying. I really need it."

He doesn't make me suffer. I hear the vibrator whir to life and then he slides it between my legs. "Fuck yourself with this, doll. And make it good. I want that pussy dripping wet for me."

I grab the vibrator and work it between my legs, my own hum of satisfaction matching its purr. Junior stretches my ass wide with the plug, pumps it in and out a dozen times before he finally lets it fully seat.

Just when I'm about to crest the peak again, he snatches the vibrator away from me. I cry out in protest, but then he slides into me and my body celebrates.

Hell, yes.

This is exactly what I need. I shudder with pleasure, crazy sounds coming out of my throat. I'm doubly full—the butt plug stretching my back hole as Junior fills and empties my pussy. It's all so glorious, so overwhelming. I beg and plead—for what, I don't know. Mercy. Climax. Who knows. I can't even understand my own words. I'm a babbling mess, delirious with pleasure, even though he's barely getting started.

"Junior, Junior, oh please. It feels so good. I need you. Oh please. More. More. Oh please give it to me. Please give it to me now."

It's embarrassing the things that come out of my mouth. Fortunately, Junior thinks it's hot. He grips my hips and pounds into me. Every time his loins hit my butt, he pushes the plug in deeper. It's way too much and not enough. I can't take him deep enough, get enough of him. Sensations roll over me in waves of pleasure, heightened need.

Junior's breath grows ragged. He curses in Italian—or maybe he's praising me, I can't tell the difference, and then he shoves in deep.

I come the moment he does, my channel squeezing around his cock, milking it for his seed.

I float off, body flushed and boneless.

"I got you a present," Junior says from somewhere out in the atmosphere. He scoops under my legs and lifts my lower half to the bed, tucked on my side.

"Mm," is all I can say.

He works the butt plug out of me and returns with a washcloth, which he uses to clean me up. I make a low purring sound.

"I got you a diamond." He holds out a tiny jewelry box. "I hope it's not too soon."

If I weren't pregnant, all of this would be too soon. But the moment I decided to give Junior another chance, I was all in. We were both all in.

I moved in here with him, he made it his job to make me happy.

I push myself up to sit and try to grab the box, but he holds it out of reach. "Tell me first if it's too soon. I can put this away and try again later."

I snort. "Seriously? You're afraid I'm going to shoot you down? After you just gave me the best orgasm of my life?"

He smiles, but still appears unsure.

"Give me my ring," I say softly. "I want it."

He cracks open the box. It's ginormous, which comes as no surprise. Junior loves to spoil me and it's probably important to him that his wife have the biggest ring. He is an alpha male after all.

Good thing I like ginormous diamond rings. I slide the emerald cut beauty on my wedding finger and beam.

"So that's a yes? You want the full proposal first?"

"It's a yes. As far as I'm concerned, you proposed to me that day in the car. But be my guest. I want the full deal."

Junior drops to one knee and holds up the jewelry box. "Desiree."

I'm surprised to hear the thickness in his voice.

"I want to be your man. I want you in my home. In my bed. In my life. Forever. I want to be the guy who makes you scream. Who protects you. Treats you like a princess. I want to be your husband, Desiree. Will you marry me?"

Tears fill my eyes and I cover my mouth to hold in the sob. "Yes," I nod, reaching for his hands to pull him up, to get closer. To touch him.

"Whenever you want to get married, I'm in. No pressure, though. I'm happy just to have you wear my ring."

"Tomorrow," I say.

"What?"

"Let's go tomorrow. We can elope." I gasp. "I know—let's go to Vegas! I heard there's this really cool casino there…."

"You wanna get married tomorrow in Vegas?" Junior's grin splits his face. "Baby, that's so easy. You sure? You don't want a big fancy wedding? I mean, fuck you can have both. Whatever you want, it's yours."

I pull him down to the bed with me. It's hard to make room, with my big belly, but we lie, nose to nose, his hand on my hip. "I just want you, Junior," I tell him.

He brushes his thumb across my cheek. "You already have me, angel. Forever."

The End

FREE BONUS SCENE with Desiree and Junior! Want to read about Desiree and Junior's interaction when she worked for his mom? I deleted a prologue because it wasn't punchy enough. It's available now to my newsletter subscribers. **Click here to get it** (If you're already a subscriber, it will be in the links at the bottom of my newsletters).

I hope you enjoyed *Joker's Wild*. If you loved it, please consider reviewing it or recommending to a friend—your reviews help indie authors so much.

Want more *Vegas Underground*? Read Nico and

Sondra's book *King of Diamonds*, Stefano and Corey's book, *Jack of Spades*, Jenna and Alex's short story, *Mafia Daddy*, Tony and Pepper's book *Ace of Hearts*, Alessia and Vlad's brava/mafia book *His Queen of Clubs* and *Dead Man's Hand*, Gio's book.

—SIGN **up for my mailing list**: https://subscribepage.com/alphastemp

--**Get text alerts of my new releases** by Texting: EZLXP55001 to 474747

--**Join Renee's Romper Room**, my Facebook reader group.

WANT MORE? READ HIS QUEEN OF CLUBS

Want More Vegas Underground?
Enjoy this excerpt from the next Vegas Underground
book, *His Queen of Clubs*

*V*lad

NO FUCKING WAY. Just when I thought I was the least lucky bastard on this continent, I catch a break.

I've been staking out the Bellissimo and Nico Tacone for two months now.

The Tacones took down my entire cell. Junior Tacone and his brothers destroyed the Chicago operation while I was back in Moscow dealing with my mother's affairs. Granted, Ivan, my idiot second, planned to take them all out and forever end their reign of influence in the Windy

City. But he failed. And six of my men were found dead in an Italian cafe.

Victor put Ivan in charge of setting up the street business, but he was too small-minded and power-hungry to make it into much. And when I was sent to join the cell, he saw me as a threat to his autonomy. I had set up a meet with Junior to get the Tacone family involved in my laundering scheme—to diversify interests—but Ivan fucked everything up. When my mother died and I had to fly home to Moscow, he used my absence to try to eliminate the Italians and take the Chicago underworld for himself.

He underestimated Junior Tacone. Six of our guys ready and waiting with guns, and Junior single-handedly shot them all dead.

I'm not heartbroken over the loss of the Chicago business. I'm more concerned with the big money operations of the *bratva*. I'm the guy who manages our laundering accounts. But killing all the men in my cell? Unacceptable. And Victor, our *pakhan,* ordered me to exact revenge, so I'm here to do exactly that.

The Tacones may have done the brotherhood a favor by taking Ivan out, but they still owe me.

Victor would go for blood. Kill everyone Junior Tacone loves. That's the way he operates. But I'm not that guy. Yes, I was raised in the violence and death of the organization, but I'm the money man.

And the Tacones have money. Plenty of it.

But it's not coming from their Chicago operation. As far as I can tell, they'd begun shutting down most of their loan sharking on the streets in the past few years, and completely closed shop since I've been back.

JOKER'S WILD

So I came to Vegas. Where they own one of the most lucrative casinos in the country. And I've been watching the two Tacones who run it, trying to figure out what my play will be. I was thinking about taking one of their women. Simple ransom. Both men are clearly devoted to their wives—girlfriends—whatever.

And things just got much easier for me. Two limos rolled up this afternoon carrying the entire Tacone family—the three brothers from Chicago, a girlfriend, a mother, and a beautiful young sister in her early twenties.

I got a gossipy cocktail waitress to tell me everything she knows. I found out they're here for Junior Tacone's wedding—a spur of the moment kind of thing. The entire top floors of the casino have been closed off for the celebration. Rumor has it Stefano, the youngest brother, might marry his fiancée at the same time.

But I don't give a shit about their marital status.

All I care about is one Tacone.

The lovely Alessia—baby sister to all five multi-millionaire brothers. I'd been trying to figure out which female to take—which brother would be most willing to pay for his woman. Now it's easy. Grab the one they all care about.

And I don't mean the mother.

Of course my decision to take Alessia over the old lady has everything to do with her model-perfect body, mile-long legs, and fucking gorgeous face. If I'm going to hole up with a Tacone female, it might as well be one who's worth looking at.

All I have to do is knock out one of the waiters before

he brings the food up to the wedding celebration and take his uniform and his place.

~

Alessia

My brother Junior is the biggest *stronzo*.

Actually, all five of my brothers are assholes, but Junior's the worst. He informed us this morning that he and his pregnant girlfriend were going to elope in Vegas.

Tonight.

Which meant we all had to fly to Vegas to see it.

Although, honestly, I wouldn't have missed this moment for the world. Even if traveling means a lot of work keeping my mother happy and my blood sugar under control. And it makes it harder to hide the fatigue caused by my kidney condition from my ever-watchful family. They don't know about it and that's how I'm going to keep it for as long as possible.

We're up in one of the Bellissimo's top floors, in a reception area with wall to wall windows overlooking Vegas. There's a Catholic priest here to marry them. And the event turned into a surprise double wedding.

Stefano, my only easy-going brother—which doesn't mean he isn't just as lethal as the rest of them—popped the question to his girlfriend Corey this morning and they decided to make it a two-fer.

"Mary, Queen of Peace, pray for us," I murmur and

cross myself in unison with the rest of the attendees and the priest.

I can't believe Junior's remarrying. Well, it's not the remarrying part that shocks me. It's the happiness that radiates from him now as he stands facing Desiree, his tough-as-nails bride. He holds both her hands in his, gazing at her like she's his whole world. Beside him stands her young son. Watching Junior's quiet bond with him brings me to tears. Junior lost his preschool daughter in a tragic accident years back and shut down completely. I never thought he'd open his heart to love again. Now he's not only got a baby on the way, but he's doing the stepdad thing.

"Isn't it beautiful?" my mom whispers tearily, squeezing my hand.

"Absolutely perfect," I agree, crying right along with my mother.

Nico's pregnant wife Sondra went all out on the decor. The hall must have ten thousand dollars worth of flowers. The pillars and real grape vines draping over the trellises make it feel like we're back in the old country.

Tasteful and extravagant, yet also low-key, the ceremony fits both couples. Only forty or so family members fill the place. It's made all the sweeter by the two pregnant bellies—Sondra and Desiree are both expecting.

I'm so thrilled to be an aunt. Children are my passion —I got my degree in early childhood education, even though I'll probably never be allowed to work. Not by my family. Not by whatever husband my family chooses for me.

It stings knowing I'll never have any of this—the love, the impromptu elopement, a family.

The expectation was always for me, as the Family princess, to endure a huge virginal church wedding to some Made man of my father or brothers' choosing. No staring into the eyes of a man who loves me. It would be an arranged marriage all the way.

I used to fervently wish for a love match. Back when I thought I'd actually marry and have children of my own. I was overjoyed when Nico got away with marrying a woman of his own choosing instead of the bride he had been promised to from the time he was ten.

I've been allowed some freedoms I never thought I'd get.

They let me go to college. I had to campaign for years just to get Junior to consider it, but in the end, he relented. The diabetes almost kept them from letting me go, though. They see me as fragile. Mamma didn't want me out of her sight. My brothers didn't think I could handle myself.

They wanted me to stay where they could protect me —in either Chicago or Las Vegas.

But in the end we all compromised. They sent me to university in the Old Country where I could be watched over by *La Famiglia.* The Sicilians. And my brother Stefano was there part of the time, too, to keep a very close eye on me.

I'm always guarded like a princess in a convent. Which doesn't mean I didn't sneak in a few experiences. I stole kisses with a nice Italian boy who took my V-card in the most respectful way possible. But when he found out I was part of the Family, he couldn't run fast enough. Which was just as well, because I wouldn't want him to be hurt.

I was just looking to live a little before it's too late.

Because what my family doesn't know is that I'm in stage three kidney failure as a result of the diabetes. I've been told having children would kill me.

So the love match and babies of my own isn't ever going to happen.

In fact, if I don't take care of myself, I may not live to see twenty-five.

~

Vlad

I RETURN to the Bellissimo with a plan and everything I need to execute it: A syringe filled with tranquilizer. Rope to tie her wrists and ankles. Tape for her mouth. Mikhail —Mika, as we call him— my twelve-year-old accomplice and the only living member of the Chicago *bratva*, to drive the getaway car.

I get off the elevator wearing the crisp Bellissimo waiter's uniform, pushing the cart I plan to carry the girl out in.

I leave the cart just outside the door and stand in the doorway, scanning the room. I keep my head down and my tattooed fingers clasped behind my back. If the Chicago-based Tacone brothers recognize me, I'll be a dead man before I can take a breath. Not that I care. If I were overly-worried about living long, I wouldn't be here. Ironically, it's my carelessness with life that always makes me come out on top.

I take risks. I'm never ruled by fear. I saw the way the *bratva* worked early on and figured out how to come out on top. I made myself indispensable. Not through violence, although I've had my fair share, but through knowledge.

I learned how to hack. How to launder. I learned to speak English, German and French. That's how I won control of all of the *bratva's* money. How I amassed a fortune. How I survived countless attacks against me. If the shit with the treacherous Sabina hadn't gone down, I'd still be on top there instead of lying low in America.

I make a mental note of every weapon-bulge in the room—at least twenty-four. Every man there is carrying a piece—even the grooms. Instead of fear, the familiar buzz of adrenaline sets my skin tingling.

A surreptitious scan of the room and I find the mafia princess. The one I will use to bring every Tacone to his knees.

The one who will learn a little humility at my hands.

I should hate my enemy's sister—should consider her an enemy too, but it's hard to hate any creature so beautiful. And it's not her fault she was born into a ruthless family.

The Italians keep their females pure. The women never participate in business. Never see blood or death.

Hell, the girl may even still be a virgin. *Blyat*, now my dick's hard. Now is not the time to get a stiffie over the woman I plan to drug and tie up. Except I'm a sick motherfucker, because that thought only gets me harder.

She's wearing a hot pink halter dress that frames and presents her youthful breasts in the most mouthwatering way. The matching pink shoes and purse probably cost a grand alone.

Fortune's smiling on me, because Alessia breaks from the group and heads for the door, like she's going to the restroom.

I move swiftly, pushing my cart into the hallway behind her, palming the syringe. I remove the false top of the cart, revealing the empty bottom, which is actually one of the Bellissimo's rolling laundry carts.

I wait until she emerges from the restroom—alone, thank fuck—and jump her from behind. If she were a man, I would just knock her out with my fist, like I did the waiter downstairs. But I can't bring myself to hit a woman, no matter how easy and effective that might be.

I catch her vanilla and roses scent as I cover her mouth and jab the hypodermic needle into her neck. She struggles against me as the drug moves through her veins. It will take at least a minute to take effect.

"Shh, *printsessa*," I murmur in her ear, keeping my grip across her arms and over her mouth, iron-tight. "Relax and you won't get hurt." My accent sounds thicker than usual. Probably because my cock just got thicker at the feel of her soft ass wriggling against it. "Easy, *zaika*. Go to sleep."

Her intoxicating floral aroma fills my nostrils as I breathe into her neck, waiting. Finally, she goes limp, her supple body sagging in my arms.

I swoop an arm under her knees and drop her into the cart, then put the top back on, arranging the tablecloth over everything. Twenty-nine seconds later I'm in the elevator. One of the Tacones' men gets on with me. I keep my face blank, but formal.

The guy doesn't look at me. I palm the knife in my pocket, ready to use it if I have to.

Finally, the guy gets off on a lower floor and a few other people get on—tourists. Nobodies. I hit the door close button and continue downstairs to the lower level.

I text Mika, *On my way*. I try to use English with him, so he'll learn to read and write it.

In position, he texts back in Russian. I shouldn't involve the kid in this shit. Hell, I shouldn't have even brought him here from Chicago. But what else was I do with him? I came back from my mother's funeral in Moscow to find six of the brotherhood dead and everyone else gone. Everyone except Mika.

He'd been living alone in the apartment building we occupied, somehow surviving. Probably a greater kindness would've been to give him to the American social care system. But I couldn't do it. He may be an annoyance, but he's one of ours, and we take care of our own. And he's working hard to prove himself useful.

In the lower level corridor, I strip off the waiter suit and put on a maintenance staff button down shirt, pull the catering top off the cart and roll it out, like I'm taking out dirty laundry. I wipe my prints from her purse and toss it in the trash.

Mika pulls around to the door and stops with a jerk. Yes, I let a twelve-year-old drive my car. I didn't even have to teach him—he already knew how. And he's damn good at it.

"Open the trunk," I mutter to him in Russian and he complies as I push the cart right up to the back of my black Jetta. I pick up the drugged Tacone princess and drop her into the trunk, then slam it shut.

Twenty-three seconds and we're out of there.

Mission accomplished. I now have all the leverage I will need against the Tacone pricks.

READ NOW

WANT FREE RENEE ROSE BOOKS?

Sign up for Renee Rose's newsletter at http://subscribepage.com/alphastemp and receive a free books! In addition to the free stories, you will also get special pricing, exclusive previews and news of new releases.

OTHER TITLES BY RENEE ROSE

Vegas Underground Mafia Romance

King of Diamonds

Mafia Daddy

Jack of Spades

Ace of Hearts

Joker's Wild

His Queen of Clubs

Dead Man's Hand

Wild Card

Chicago Bratva

The Director

More Mafia Romance

Her Russian Master

The Don's Daughter

Mob Mistress

The Bossman

Contemporary
Daddy Rules Series

Fire Daddy

Hollywood Daddy

Stepbrother Daddy

Master Me Series

Her Royal Master

Her Russian Master

Her Marine Master

Yes, Doctor

Double Doms Series

Theirs to Punish

Theirs to Protect

Holiday Feel-Good

Scoring with Santa

Saved

Other Contemporary

Black Light: Valentine Roulette

Black Light: Roulette Redux

Black Light: Celebrity Roulette

Black Light: Roulette War

Punishing Portia (written as Darling Adams)

The Professor's Girl

Safe in his Arms

Paranormal

Wolf Ranch Series

Rough

Wild

Feral

Savage

Fierce

Ruthless

Wolf Ridge High Series

Alpha Bully

Alpha Knight

Bad Boy Alphas Series

Alpha's Temptation

Alpha's Danger

Alpha's Prize

Alpha's Challenge

Alpha's Obsession

Alpha's Desire

Alpha's War

Alpha's Mission

Alpha's Bane

Alpha's Secret

Alpha's Prey

Alpha's Sun

Midnight Doms

Alpha's Blood

His Captive Mortal

Alpha Doms Series

The Alpha's Hunger

The Alpha's Promise

The Alpha's Punishment

Other Paranormal

The Winter Storm: An Ever After Chronicle

Sci-Fi

Zandian Masters Series

His Human Slave

His Human Prisoner

Training His Human

His Human Rebel

His Human Vessel

His Mate and Master

Zandian Pet

Their Zandian Mate

His Human Possession

Zandian Brides

Night of the Zandians

Bought by the Zandians

Mastered by the Zandians

Zandian Lights

Kept by the Zandian

Claimed by the Zandian

Other Sci-Fi

The Hand of Vengeance

Her Alien Masters

Regency

The Darlington Incident

Humbled

The Reddington Scandal

The Westerfield Affair

Pleasing the Colonel

Western

His Little Lapis

The Devil of Whiskey Row

The Outlaw's Bride

Medieval

Mercenary

Medieval Discipline

Lords and Ladies

The Knight's Prisoner

Betrothed

Held for Ransom

The Knight's Seduction

The Conquered Brides (5 book box set)

Renaissance

Renaissance Discipline

ABOUT RENEE ROSE

USA TODAY BESTSELLING AUTHOR RENEE ROSE loves a dominant, dirty-talking alpha hero! She's sold over a million copies of steamy romance with varying levels of kink. Her books have been featured in USA Today's *Happily Ever After* and *Popsugar*. Named Eroticon USA's Next Top Erotic Author in 2013, she has also won *Spunky and Sassy's* Favorite Sci-Fi and Anthology author and *The Romance Reviews* Best Historical Romance. She's hit the *USA Today* list seven times with her Wolf Ranch books and various anthologies.

Please follow her on:
   Bookbub | Goodreads

Renee loves to connect with readers!
www.reneeroseromance.com
reneeroseauthor@gmail.com

Printed in Great Britain
by Amazon